GW0065744Ø

YAEL INOKAI was born in 1989 in Basel and lives in Berlin. She won the 2018 Swiss Literature Prize for her second novel, *Mahlstrom*. Her third novel, *A Simple Intervention*, was longlisted for the 2022 German Book Prize and is her first work to be translated into English.

MARIELLE SUTHERLAND was born in 1976 in Hartlepool. She has a PhD in German and is a translator at the German Historical Institute London. Her publications include the selected poems of Rainer Maria Rilke (co-translated with Susan Ranson) and *Rulantica: Hidden Island* by Michaela Hanauer. Marielle Sutherland was awarded the 2023 Peirene Stevns Translation Prize.

A SIMPLE INTERVENTION

Yael Inokai

Translated from the German
by Marielle Sutherland

PEIRENE

First published in 2024 by
Peirene Press Ltd
The Studio
10 Palace Yard Mews
Bath BA1 2NH

© 2022 Hanser Berlin in der Carl Hanser
Verlag GmbH & Co. KG, München

This translation © Marielle Sutherland

ISBN 978-1-908670-87-8

Designed by Orlando Lloyd
Cover illustration by Tessa Mackenzie
Typeset by Tetragon, London
Printed and bound by TJ Books, Padstow, Cornwall

The translation of this work was supported by the Peirene
Stevns Translation Prize, which was established in 2018
with the generous support of Martha Stevns.

A SIMPLE
INTERVENTION

October. A time for ghosts. I see myself in the mirror as a young woman again. Conviction in my eyes. Unclouded by doubt. I'm in my mid-twenties, and I understand the world.

Later, when I knew more, I longed to go back to that time. When my belief in my work protected me.

I was a nurse in a hospital pioneering new kinds of interventions. These interventions were meant to free people from psychological disorders and release them into a new future – a real future, not just a continued existence.

I hung on to this hope. After all, our work wasn't exactly lacking in hopelessness. Often enough, there was nothing more we could do. Nothing more. Other nurses would never have put it like that. We were there right through to the end, of course, and beyond. But for me, this verdict tore open an abyss every time.

I was the one who assisted the doctor during the intervention. He navigated his instruments to the affected area of the brain and neutralized it. The patients were awake during the procedure. That's how we made sure we didn't damage any healthy tissue. I kept them occupied and took away their fear. I called this compassion. I told myself: *I can do this because I have compassion.*

7

It was a simple intervention. The after-effects could be painful, but they were only temporary. Then something new would begin. That's what I was taught. And I clung to it.

MARIANNE

1

The first impression of the day: rain on the window. Footsteps. The clatter of bikes being pulled off stands and loaded up before the first of us got on and rode off into the morning.

The nurses' halls of residence were on the edge of town. The road on the right led down to the industrial estate. We always went left, past the terraced houses with their steeply pitched roofs, then through the wood until we got to the hospital. At the halfway point was a turn-off towards the town.

The house had its louder and quieter hours. But never silence. Sometimes a dream tore my night to shreds and I'd lie there in the dark, listening to the building. I'd hear the water rushing through the pipes behind the wall and think of the flat I'd grown up in, which for most of my childhood I'd believed was made of paper. I'd lie there listening to the others falling into their beds, each tired body ten times heavier than when awake, and I'd realize how much a bed has to support: bones and flesh and blood, and all a person has seen.

Just before the alarm clock went off, I'd fall back to sleep. Those few minutes always catapulted me far away, and I'd need a few more to get back again. I would stretch my toes from under the blanket, then my fingers – the only part of me that wasn't buried was my head. My shoes were never where I thought I'd put them. Each time, my feet found the cold floor. The shock struck my soles like lightning. *Come on now, no dawdling.*

Our room was furthest from the toilets. They were at the end of a long corridor, which was narrow and cold, with two windows opening straight out onto the courtyard. Every morning, I did my shivery little dance as I waited there in the queue to relieve myself.

A sour smell hovered over the washbasins. Arms were raised, armpits wiped with flannels. The stench of uneasy dreams, too, hung in the air, as poor souls tried to rub the sandy residue of sleep from their eyes.

I washed my hands and slapped cold water onto my cheeks, forehead and mouth. I drank, then spat out the night that always lay furred on my tongue.

After the bathroom ritual, I put on one of my dresses. I chose according to the weather. Their purpose was to get me from door to door. I was careless with them. Other people pointed out the tears, holes and stains.

Breakfast in the dining room was a brief affair. Five minutes were enough. Hardly any of us were hungry at that time of day. There were some, like me, who were conditioned to eat when food was there. They ate the porridge and apples impassively and were grateful for the weak coffee. There were those who devoured two or three portions, storing it up for later. There were also a few lively types who treated breakfast like a proper meal.

No one left it untouched. A nurse with an empty stomach was no good to anyone.

Back in my room, the only thing left to do was put on my thin jacket. I closed the door behind me and joined the stream of nurses making their way down the steps, putting on their shoes at the bottom and heading towards their bikes. I reached straight for the familiar handlebars. We got on and set off. We said nothing. The bikes performed their own rattling concert.

I'd been working at the hospital for eight years. I couldn't imagine any other world. Or any routine other than this, among nurses getting ready for their duties.

2

I was proud of who I was when I wore the uniform. I remember exactly how it felt in the hospital changing room, morning after morning: the starched, white material on my skin, fastening the buttons, pinning on the watch, putting on the cap. The person I became as I did so. The version of myself I liked most.

My ward was on the fifth floor. I'd completed most of my training there, and then I'd stayed.

Before the start of the shift, I washed my hands. They no longer flinched under the cold water. They'd got used to the constant washing. For the first few months, they were red and cracked, incessantly sore, screaming at me as I lay in bed at night trying to sleep. But the body can get used to just about anything.

Then came the handover. The night nurses tried not to let the past few hours show on their faces. They looked at me, and gave me nothing more than a room number. A few looked right through me, the abyss in their eyes.

Nothing but a room number. Someone had died. Every time, there was that disbelief at the back of my throat.

When I entered the rooms, they'd already been cleaned. In the beginning, it was my job to remove the traces of the deceased. I'd scrub death out of the room and restore order to the things left behind. Back then, each book, each photo evoked a feeling of nausea. I was glad when that passed.

Then I was put in charge of the suitcases. I had to deal with them before the millstones of my day ground into motion. Death was a matter for the night. Only rarely did anyone dare be the exception.

The suitcases were always waiting for me on the table. Everything the deceased had taken out on arrival had been packed up again. I undid the buckles and checked whether this had been done carefully. Then I closed the cases, pulled them down from the table and took them to the lost property room. We kept them there for six weeks. If no one claimed them, we gave them to charity.

Now and again, I noticed the cases had been collected. I saw women, men and children in the corridors. They sat on the benches with the open cases, their hands buried in jumpers and dresses, holding a book someone had been reading a few days before. At a loss, they rummaged through pictures, papers and perfume bottles. Perhaps they were amazed everything was still there. Or perhaps these people they thought they'd known so well had become mysteries once more.

Other suitcases were left behind. I didn't want to, but I became good at guessing in advance which ones these would be. I put these suitcases on the shelf right at the back, so I didn't have to see them every time I opened the door. I still hoped someone would come and take them, just as I hoped someone would come and sit in the empty chairs by the beds for a few minutes, hold out a hand and say hello. It's no more difficult than breathing. And yet there's nothing more difficult.

The older nurses said: *Work with time. Time will be on your side. Not today, not tomorrow, but eventually, when you've been here long enough and you've lost count of the number of people you've cared for.*

In principle, it was easy. Each of us was capable of putting it all behind us – the days, months and years filled with all the doubts they held for a young person. Eventually, the pull of time would be strong enough. All you had to do was keep going.

The nurses said: *Get up every morning like you did the morning before. Eat, drink your coffee, get on your bike, ride to work, carry out your duties, and you'll keep a level head. If you do things over and over again, you'll get better at them, until the work is inside you. Just like your lungs are inside you. Just like your heart is inside you. That's when you'll stop fearing that something will affect you too much. You'll start seeing the bigger picture instead of individual faces. Nausea? Don't worry – it'll pass.*

One time, a suitcase dropped to the floor. Its owner had travelled a long way and she'd run out of strength over the last few metres. All I heard was the dull thud as it hit the floor, but I knew she'd be standing outside in the corridor, waiting for me.

One suitcase among thousands, with two books, two photos, a pen, a pencil, a passport, a dress, a cardigan, a nightdress, underwear, slippers, a brush, perfume, nail polish, a key and a pack of cards.

The older nurses said I should work with time. It would free me from such images.

Sarah never believed that. 'I'll never forget my patients' faces. What makes you think time is on our side?'

3

There was a book. I'd opened it countless times to read it to my sister. 'Once upon a time...' The story of a vixen who fell asleep in the basket of a hot-air balloon and accidentally flew round the world.

As a child, Bibi wouldn't have any other bedtime story, only ever this one. I could even use it to guide her back to bed when she was sleepwalking.

She was born five years after me, to everyone's surprise. For a while, she shared a room with me and my older brother, Wilm – the flat had only two bedrooms, and one belonged indisputably to my parents. But one day, Wilm packed his things, announced he'd never survive growing up with two sisters at such close quarters, and moved into the kitchen. Every morning, he folded up his bed, and by day it served as a bench where all three of us sat to eat at the table. Bibi and I were only allowed to take a seat once he'd thrown the bedspread over it.

Bibi often visited him when she was sleepwalking. Wilm could tell the story of the vixen without so much as a glance at the book. Sometimes, half-asleep, I could hear him. First, the startled cry when our sister appeared by his bed in the middle of the night, her eyes vacant because she was somewhere else entirely. Then the words, his warm voice croaking occasionally.

When I moved out to start my training, Bibi slipped the tattered book into my suitcase when I wasn't looking. I only found it a few weeks after I arrived at the nurses' halls. The onset of winter called for a thick woolly cardigan. She'd wrapped the book inside. With a message on the first page: *So you'll find your way back to me.*

4

The woman and I were both twenty-five. I saw in her notes that our birthdays were only three days apart. I kept that in mind.

Her father was running late. So to begin with she stood by herself in the hallway, looking around. She wasn't shaking, and there was no fear in her eyes. People can get the better of these things, but the body can't be outwitted altogether. Hands become clammy, losing their grip on the luggage they've been clutching. And the suitcase betrays with a loud thud how much is packed inside. Never because its owner expects to be staying a long time. A heavy suitcase wants to bring the feeling of home, with all its superfluous knick-knacks, into a strange room, to make staying there just about bearable.

She arrived in the morning. I already had one intervention behind me. The patient was now drifting slowly, and without complications, out of anaesthetic stupor and back into her aching body. The doctor operated in the mornings – that was his favourite way to start the day. He also liked the nights, the emergencies. He didn't grumble when he was called out to the hospital in the small hours. But he didn't cope well in the afternoons. Those hours when the morning had grown weary and was listlessly awaiting the break of dusk. That's when the doctor withdrew to his room and did his paperwork.

The woman had picked her suitcase back up off the floor. She was unmistakably an Ellerbach. Tall, with an upright posture and a face that could never have belonged to a poor person. This face went with money and a certain recognition in the world. A family of industrialists, known all over town. Their factories were on the industrial estate behind the nurses' halls. They were also a family of philanthropists. This was at the heart of their work, something the father never tired of emphasizing in public. The company's foundation funded school and library renovations and scholarships for gifted students. It turned private land into public parks. The Ellerbachs were inscribed on the town. Their names were on plaques all around it.

I thought about this when I saw the woman in the flesh for the first time. I knew her face from the newspaper. There were four of them, the Ellerbach children. Three brothers and her. She was the youngest. Her name was Marianne.

As I extended my hand towards her, she handed me her suitcase, not mistaking the gesture for a greeting, as others did.

'Hello. Are you here to fetch me?' At first, she didn't look at me at all. She was still studying her surroundings. Her eyes followed two nurses walking past us. This gave me time to form a first impression and swallow my surprise at how little she stood out despite everything. 'It's a nice day, isn't it?' Her gaze lingered on a half-open door to a room. She tried to peer inside. 'But it's so... white in here. Doesn't it bother you?'

She abandoned her reconnaissance and turned to me, looking straight at me for the first time. I too was tall. She hadn't been expecting that. With others, she was always looking down at the tops of their heads, but she was eye level with me.

'You're tall,' she observed, laughing so loudly that the two nurses in the corridor turned to look at us.

'My name's Meret,' I said.

'That suits you.'

There was a blue box. It was my toolbox for interventions of this kind. It was full of things to keep people occupied: books, pictures, puzzles, card games, matches, a flip book, a little concertina. Most of them had been left behind – I took them from the suitcases before they went to charity.

These things were for me too. They gave me something to hold on to. I felt confident when I took the blue box from the cupboard and brought it to my patients.

Choosing something for Marianne Ellerbach was easy. When she opened her case, I saw a pack of cards between the brush and the perfume. That's how I knew she'd like the pack in the box. It was a particularly beautiful deck, with a delicate pattern.

'I noticed our birthdays are only three days apart,' I said. 'You were born first, on September the twelfth, and then it was my turn, on the fifteenth.'

'Really?' She stopped arranging her things and, without the slightest hesitation, sat down on the bed, jiggling her feet from side to side. I realized she had so much freedom. Wherever she went, she could simply sit down. She never stopped to ask herself whether a space was meant for her.

We both looked over at the door, expecting her father and the doctor to come in. I knew so much about her, and she knew nothing at all about me. I knew about her episodes. There was a rage within her that could grow and grow until it detonated, battering everything around it with savage words, screaming and violence. This rage came on quickly. If you were anywhere in its vicinity, you rarely had enough time to get to safety. When it happened, her three brothers' physical superiority was of no use to them. Marianne's rage was bigger than they were.

I'd seen plenty of photos of the Ellerbach family in the local newspaper. The father surrounded by his three sons, his daughter and his wife – a fixed point of orientation for everything in the picture, even the furniture. Marianne was always standing beside the same brother, the youngest, one and a half years older than her. He looked astonishingly like his father.

In our family photos, Bibi was always standing beside Wilm. Always beside her big brother, who had his father's hair, nose and mouth. But not his eyes.

While Marianne's eyes wandered slowly around the room, I watched her. You couldn't tell she had episodes. Certainly there was that loud laugh, and the restlessness in her limbs. And she was childlike. The way she stared so unashamedly at whatever she liked, anything or anyone, she could have been a good fifteen years younger. Apart from that, there was no sign of her disorder. But of course, the seemingly normal can take a turn. I knew that by now.

When her father came in, she didn't stand up. 'Morning,' he said to his daughter. She returned his greeting with a dispassionate nod. She was probably the only person in the world who didn't intuitively stand up when he entered the room. I myself took a step backwards – it was automatic.

She let him kiss her on the forehead. He placed his hand briefly on the back of her head and drew her towards him. 'Now, now,' he murmured. For a moment, maybe a second, he wasn't an Ellerbach. He didn't fill the entire room. He was just a father being affectionate towards his daughter. She carried on jiggling her feet from side to side, not a grown woman but a child surrendering to this affection.

When the doctor arrived, I was surprised to see that even he seemed paler next to the Ellerbachs. Like a photo whose colours had faded. He was usually impressive in his appearance. It wasn't anything to do with physical attributes. The doctor was neither tall nor broad-shouldered, nor was his face in any way distinctive. But he knew who he was. And it was this certainty that won everyone over.

'Good morning,' said the doctor, and when the customary response didn't come, he turned to me, indicated the file in my hand and instructed me to 'Take notes, please.' He might as well have said 'Breathe, please.'

Marianne's father had specifically asked that the doctor meet her on her own first, without his assistants. A special request for special patients. Made by anyone else, it would have been indignantly refused. But this time the doctor even sat down on a chair so he could be at eye level with his patient. 'These episodes—' he began.

'That's not me!'

He nodded, grateful for the interjection. 'No, it's not you. Of course not. Which is why I'd like to help you get rid of this rage. If you will allow me.'

She nodded hesitantly.

'There's something inside you, and I'm going to put it to sleep. It won't bother you any more. And then it will sleep forever. It's as simple as that.'

The doctor explained the procedure to her, leaving out any words that might cause her unnecessary anxiety. Her father had been given a different version. And the staff yet another. But what he was saying here was no less true. As simple as his explanation was, it was a delicate undertaking. Fear made things delicate.

The woman listened, cutting in to ask, 'Will it hurt?'

'No, it won't hurt.'

For the first time since the others had come into the room, she sought my gaze. I nodded affirmatively. No pain. Pain came later. But we didn't talk about that right then.

The doctor pivoted back to her episodes. He started with these and ended on these, so she wouldn't forget how serious her disorder was, or even consider that she might be able to carry on living like this. 'You have to think of your disorder as a flood tide,' he said. 'The sea ebbs, then it comes back again. Just as surely as it ebbs, it will come back again. The further it ebbs, the higher the water will rise when it comes back.' He waited, trying to gauge from

Marianne's eyes whether the metaphor had had any effect. 'Eventually, this flood tide will drag everything with it. It will leave us with no option but to treat it with medication, so we can protect you and your loved ones.'

He pulled out two photos from among his papers and showed them to her. A young woman, the same age as her. And the same woman, a little older, after the medication had done its damage.

Marianne gave the photos a perfunctory glance. They didn't give her the intended fright. But she would think about them later, when the doubts grew within her, and with them the urge to get out of bed and leave.

'It is important that you are awake during the procedure,' the doctor said finally. He didn't always broach the subject so cautiously. There'd been occasions when, pushed for time, he'd simply brought it up just before leaving the room and I was left to deal with it. But not in her case. She was given a precise, judicious introduction in carefully chosen words. 'You'll help us navigate. You'll be present, but without pain and without fear. You'll be there. Your eyes will be open—'

'No,' she said. Her voice started to crack. 'I don't want that. I want to sleep, and when I wake up, I want it all to be over.'

'It's *like* sleeping.'

'So why can't I sleep properly then?'

'It'll be quicker than going to the dentist's,' said her father.

You could always count on that: a relative trying to be helpful but sabotaging everything at the last minute.

'The dentist's!' She clasped her hand to her jaw, her eyes moving frantically between doctor and door. Something was rattling inside her. Bad memories. She wanted to run away.

'We'll play cards,' I said. I put the file to one side, took the deck out of the blue box and held it out to her. Her father looked at me for the first time. He hadn't noticed me before. I was just another object in this room.

'I can play cards while it's happening?' Her hand dropped from her jaw. She picked up the cards and fanned them out in her hand. It was a familiar gesture. That would make it easier. Skin has its own memory. It can always bring us back.

'Yes. Or sing. Some patients sing. If there's a song you like… we can sing that too.'

The fear in her eyes seemed to subside a little. She turned over her hand to take a closer look at the back of the cards.

'Guess what?' she said, turning to her father. 'The nurse was born only three days after me.'

5

The brain is a map. Everything I am is located there. I grew into my profession with this image in my head. It made sense. Tumours crush optic nerves, leading to blindness. Neurological diseases erode people's memories, their language, their motor skills, little by little, until their hands can't even keep a grip any more. These diseases can be located. Why should it be any different with psychological disorders? Why shouldn't we be able to remove these too, and release people into a life worth living?

It took no time at all to complete the intervention. We were usually in theatre no longer than an hour. It was simple, and like everything simple, it had taken a long time to develop and refine. The right tools, the right hands that knew how to use the tools, the right voices to guide the procedure. And the failures, of course. No one liked to talk about those. But failures drove development.

The doctor had to find the affected area and put it to sleep, like a sick animal. That was his job. Mine was to keep the patients occupied. I was to distract them from what was happening and keep them interacting with me. As long as they stayed awake, we knew the doctor and his instruments had found the right place. I was attentive to every word and every glance. I took away the patients' fear, which could return regardless of what the sedatives were telling the body to do.

That's how we worked together.

At that time, the developments were met with distrust from many quarters. After all, the intervention hadn't been tried and tested yet. The first few times, the brain tissue wasn't put to sleep but incised. 'Like cutting a cable' was how the doctor had put it when he told me about the early days of the procedure. Had that been necessary? Couldn't they have got to where we are now another way? His position on this was clear. And in all the years I knew him, he never deviated from it. 'Progress can be painful. Things get worse before they get better. That's just how it is.'

That's just how it is. That was just one of the doors the doctor swung shut and disappeared behind. Sometimes it was his office door. Sometimes the door to his eyes. I envied him that.

As far as the intervention itself was concerned, opinion was also divided among the nurses on our ward. If they had an opinion at all. Some of them had given up holding any kind of opinion. Rules and regulations were always comfortable to fall back on. Opinions weren't.

6

Marianne remained placid throughout the afternoon. She'd unpacked her case and slipped into a lightweight dress. I checked in on her every hour and would find her reading or standing by the window watching the goings-on outside. Eventually she asked, 'Will you play a round of cards with me, Sister?'

'You can call me Meret.'

But she was not the kind of person who needed to remember names.

Once the period of acclimatization was over and the preparations began, she said to the doctor, 'Do it quickly. There's a concert at the end of the week, and I don't want to miss it.'

'A concert?' replied the doctor, sounding genuinely interested. He didn't say, 'That's wishful thinking, Frau Ellerbach. After the intervention, we'll have to tiptoe up to you and whisper. A fly in the room will sound like a jackhammer. A concert? You'd be better putting that off until next month.'

She didn't react to his question. Instead she said, 'And make a thorough job of it. Only the diseased bit. I'll still need the rest.'

It was a short-lived rebellion. She was soon lying in bed. A nurse had plaited her hair into pigtails. The drug the doctor had injected her with was now circulating in her blood and taking effect.

I said goodbye to her at the end of my shift. I placed my hand on her shoulder and told her what time to expect me tomorrow. 'Get the cards ready for a rematch,' I added. 'You were brutal with me this afternoon. I can't let you get away with that.'

When her gaze met mine, the rage rose within it, glinting in her eyes, tensing her jaw. 'Please stay,' she managed to say. Or at least that's what I could make out through her clenched teeth. I sat down by her bed. She was breathing faster. She snorted. Her limbs stiffened. Her hand shot out and clutched the fabric of my uniform. I allowed her this. There was nothing more I could do.

That's when her rage detonated. A blast went through her body, sending her arms and legs into spasms. Her breathing faltered. Her forehead broke into a sweat. Her pulse was racing. She opened her mouth to scream, but her voice lacked the necessary strength, giving out only a few distorted sounds.

Her hand clung on, pulling me so close that I picked up the stale scent slowly permeating through her perfume. The same stale scent as all the others who lay in these beds. The stale scent that clung to me too, even after I'd freed myself from my uniform. When I found it on me, I went straight under the shower and soaped my neck, behind my ears, in the hollows of my knees and between my toes and buttocks. I wasn't even as thorough when it came to washing off death.

Marianne's voice was gaining strength. Soon it would be audible in the corridor. I wanted to bend over her and smother the sound. I didn't want anyone to come and do anything about it. Her rage needed to run its course.

Then she fell silent. The spasms ebbed. She fought for air. Her eyes found mine again, this time unobstructed by rage.

'It's okay,' I said softly, 'it's okay. It'll soon be over.' She relaxed her grip. I loosened her hand from my uniform and gave it a little squeeze. Then I stood up, soaked a cloth in cold water and wiped the sweat from her brow. Her breathing calmed. She murmured something.

'Sorry? I can't understand what you're saying.' I leaned towards her and put my ear to her mouth.

'My brother,' she said, 'he plays this game.' She was about to explain, but a residual twitch of rage went through her, severing her words.

I straightened up a little. 'Just stay calm. I'm here. Take your time.'

'My brother plays this game.' Marianne was trying to calm herself now. She folded her hands together and closed her eyes. She took a deep breath, held it for a moment, then blew out through her mouth.

So she has her own tools, I thought. They might be ridiculous compared with what we are offering her. But they aren't nothing. A deep, focused breath is never nothing.

'He does it deliberately. He says... he is clumsy.' Her hand came out again, but instead of reaching for me she took hold of a book on her bedside table and dropped it on the floor. 'Like this. That's how things fall in our house...

32

glasses and vases. Only the most expensive things. The glowing ends of his cigarettes burn... holes in his suits. He treads on nails.' She turned her head towards me. 'Do you have any brothers or sisters?'

'One brother and one sister.'

'Do they play games too?'

I bent down to pick up the book. Her eyes followed me. 'They used to, a long time ago,' I said.

'Why don't you tell me about them?' She patted the blanket. But it wasn't really a request.

7

The laws of our flat:

1. Take off your shoes before coming in.
2. Hang up your coat behind the door.
3. Wash your hands. With soap. With a brush if you have dirt under your fingernails. Otherwise someone else will do it for you. And you know how that feels.
4. Don't shout *Hello* in the hallway. Don't announce: *I'm HOME* like the neighbours do. Greet your mother and your father by going to them and looking them in the eye. Or at least by looking at their closed bedroom door.
5. Only your parents are allowed to close their bedroom door.
6. Your father may also close it on your mother.
7. Eat when food is there.
8. Don't speak at mealtimes during the week.
9. The order for using the bathroom: your father, your mother, your brother; what you negotiate with your sister is up to you.

10. Everything has its place, not just the shoes outside the door. Every object. Every one of you.
11. When you feel things taking a turn, look away quickly, avoid eye contact.
12. If you miss the right moment, don't look away, don't cower, don't walk out the door. And tell your sister, even if you've already told her a hundred times, that pulling the blanket over her head won't help. Just hold out and wait for it to pass. That makes it go quicker. It will calm down. It always calms down.
13. Say goodbye before you leave.
14. Never part on bad terms.

My sister played a game. She reached for the tension in the air, took hold of it with both hands and stretched it.

My sister was watchful. She never missed a single twitch of the eye or furrowed brow. She always knew exactly when things would take a turn. We all knew. In fact, we also had the ability to avert it. Most of the time, at least. We could see it coming. We knew when it was better to nod silently, even though everything inside us was screaming, when it was better to move, even though everything inside us wanted to stay still, and when to turn to stone, even though our legs were trying to run away. It wasn't hard. When you know how it goes, it isn't hard. Family is like an inoculation. Something you're inured to.

My sister played a game. She said, 'Guess what? That neighbour was cooking stark naked last night. Have a look! Maybe she's doing it again today!' She got up from the dining table and pulled aside the curtain, that carefully fitted piece of fabric which made us better than them over there. Our kitchen windows were two metres apart. A mother lived in the opposite flat with her grown-up son. They cooked a great deal, and dangerously – something was always burning. Then they'd open the window and fill the entire air shaft with smoke. And they argued like that too. A great deal, and loudly, and then they'd open the window to let out all their aggravation.

'Bibiana!' my father cried. 'Close that curtain right away!' But Bibi stood still, took hold of the tension in the air and stretched it. She rode out the minute in which my father's patience wore thinner and thinner, his rage rose from the pit of his stomach to his head and his fingers began to tremble. The fork fell from his hand. My sister knew that was the final sign, the last chance to avert it. She let the opportunity pass. My brother tried to intervene. He pulled the fabric out of her hand and closed the curtain again. But my father had directed the order at her, not him. Silence fell over the kitchen. My father stood up, leaned over the table, drew back his arm and slapped my sister across the face. The blow reverberated and the cutlery clattered – my father could never hit anyone without his body knocking against something else. The world was simply too small for him, even for his beatings. 'Now sit down this minute,' he ordered.

My sister thought about it. Did she want to keep playing the game? She could withstand a lot. Her body was different to mine. For her, taking a beating was a distinction. Unlike me, for whom it was unpleasant but unavoidable.

Misdemeanours have consequences; everyone knows that. My sister liked to provoke our father. She didn't only want to be beaten for accidental transgressions. She wanted him to know that if he lost control, it had been *her* choice. She hated those times when she gave in and he said, 'You very nearly felt the back of my hand there.' That was an insult to her. She could hardly bear it.

Today, she'd had enough. Today, she didn't have the strength to keep playing the game. I could see that. She was my sister, and I'd known her since the day she was born. The blow had exhausted her. She sat down. Her right cheek was glowing red with her little triumph.

8

I'd been at the hospital for six and a half years before the doctor invited me into his office, 'for a word'. I'd already heard that he was working on a new kind of intervention. Nurses were saying it was a radical treatment for people with psychological disorders. The doctor had brought it from the psychiatric institutions to the hospital, with the aim of developing it here properly.

At that time, I rarely had direct contact with the doctor. I reported to the older nurses, and they were the ones who gave me my instructions. Nonetheless, I knew about his quirks. Without even looking up, I knew him by his gait. He didn't hurry around like the rest of us. He had the resolve of a man whose time was precious.

'How did you like it in theatre?' he asked. He sat slightly askew on his chair. We all knew he had a bad back. It was, after all, essential to know such things about one's superiors in order to read situations correctly. The nurses all knew what the hunched shoulders meant, the white knuckles on the edge of the clipboard. They heard the barely audible cracks in his voice when it asked for something. They'd learned not to flinch in these moments. They'd learned to stay upright, avoid unnecessary noises, shake out their hands to stop their own bodies stiffening with unease.

'You mean during my training?'

He blinked. His way of nodding when it was too painful to move.

'I liked it.' I wasn't lying. I understood why nurses were attracted to this kind of work. In the second year of my training, I'd attended operations, one under the doctor's direction. I'd been amazed by the precise timing of everything. In theatre, even the smallest manoeuvre was orchestrated. And the person on the table – who, when awake, could be the most difficult thing of all – slept.

'And you've never thought of transferring?'

'No.'

'Why not?'

I returned his gaze. I didn't understand the genuine interest it harboured.

'Well, you're thorough. You follow procedures. You work quickly and calmly when required. You love medicine and believe in progress. At least that's what the ward manager says about you. And, in my experience, the ward manager is always right.' He cleared his throat. 'So that raises the question – why aren't you where the progress is happening? Why work on the ward when you could be in theatre?'

Most surgeons had a quick temper. They were known for their outbursts, and they cultivated them. We knew exactly what to expect. Coarse insults and bluster followed simple rules.

It was different with the doctor. Calmer. I'd witnessed that myself. He simply asked for his instruments, dedicated himself to his patient, gave instructions. He never shouted. He never even broke out in a sweat. When I came out of theatre that day and washed my hands, I realized I was shaking. So calm had it been in there that my body didn't know what to do with itself.

'I'd miss the nuances. In dealing with people.'

'Tell me about these nuances.'

Something within me laughed. I bit my lip to stop it coming out.

'Give me an example.'

It wasn't customary for the doctors to ask us about our work. Not so openly. They usually did their best to conceal the fact that they needed our knowledge.

'Let's say a patient is hovering between life and death.' I slid forward on my chair a little. 'And I know, as the guidelines state, that I should address them by their surname because... first names are reserved for us nurses.'

The corners of his mouth twitched. A smile? I feared so. I didn't want him to smile at me. I didn't want him to like me. I'd been able to avoid anything like that so far. Being liked by a doctor rarely ended well.

'But I'll ask this patient for her first name. Or I'll look for her first name in the files if she can't tell me. I'll use it when I'm caring for her.'

'Why?'

'Because... a surname is an attribution. Something she moves through the world with. But her first name is what people have always called her. Before she could even speak. It's inside her. Deeper than...' I fell silent. Expressing these thoughts in front of him felt like I was revealing a secret.

A childish secret. The doctor had the power to tear it to pieces in mid-air – a power I'd just given him.

He placed his hand on his chest. 'So, if I were lying here, half-dead, and you called me Jonas, would you be calling me back to the land of the living?'

I looked down at his desk. A photo of his daughters stood there. Whenever he called them he always shouted into the receiver, as if the line to his house was particularly bad. You could hear him sometimes through the closed door as you passed by. That's when you knew he was talking to one of his girls.

'I certainly wouldn't call you Jonas. Whatever the circumstances.'

He folded his arms. 'I'd like to know more about these nuances. Soon. We'll talk again.'

And we did. After that, he often invited me into his office after my shift. He had someone bring me coffee. He said he was interested in compassion. He believed that research had neglected the human factor in medical treatment. He wanted to find out more about it.

I filled him in on the nurses' different attitudes. That compassion was frowned upon by many of them. That some judged it to be dangerous. And that others were convinced it was an essential part of our work. It was the older nurses who influenced attitudes on their respective wards. On ours, the belief prevailed that it was a good thing. Indispensable. That's how I'd been trained.

Sitting in his office, he nearly always began our conversation with an observation: 'I noticed that at the end of your

41

shift, you took the time to write a letter for the patient. You wrote it, but the patient had to dictate it. You insisted on this. But it would probably have been easy for you to formulate this letter yourself.' He said, 'You commit details to memory. A preference for milk in tea. An enthusiasm for films.' His observations were always followed by the same question: 'Why? Try to explain it to me in a basic way, as if I had no idea about anything.'

I grew accustomed to the hours in his office. It was a place where I was given privileges. 'What would you say to me releasing you from your night shifts? Then you'll always be there when I have questions or want to show you something.'

Sometimes, in the middle of a conversation about medicine, he'd give a dismissive wave and ask me instead about my family. 'A wild child,' was his diagnosis the first time I told him about Bibiana and one of her escapades. 'My youngest can't be tamed either. The older siblings hold the world together, and the little ones trample it to pieces. That seems to be a law of nature.' He reached for the telephone. 'I wish I could split myself in half, then we could continue our conversation into the night. But my daughter isn't at home today. It's the first night she's sleeping elsewhere, and I promised she'd still hear my voice.' He dialled the number. He looked down at his desk, briefly deprived of his usual certainty. 'To be honest, I'm a little nervous myself. She's sleeping at her aunt's. It's not as if she's on a trip round the world. I really hope it's a good line.' He raised his hand to bid farewell and I stood up and left the room, closing the door behind me. 'Hello?' I heard him shouting as I paused in the corridor.

I stood still. I didn't want to disappear into the evening. In this office, with him, things became possible. These things were beyond anything I could have accomplished on my own. They were the opposite of hopelessness.

He laughed, then asked his daughter whether he should tell her a story. 'Or do you want the one you've heard a hundred times before? Okay then, I don't mind...'

I sat down on the bench in front of his office and waited until he'd hung up. He didn't invite me in again. And I got used to the fact that it was always he who put an end to our conversations.

9

I was to be my own toolkit. The doctor assumed that would be enough. That's how we got through the first few interventions.

The patients were put into a state in which they were fully conscious but felt no pain. They sat on the operating chair with their upper body tilted back. The doctor and his two assistants stood by the head, and I stood opposite so the patients could always see me. I sang songs. I spelled out words with them. I made up simple puzzles for them to solve.

My fifth patient was young. Eighteen, according to her passport, which she carried with her in a small, lightweight suitcase. She'd been held in a juvenile detention centre before she came to us.

The conversation with the doctor about the impending intervention was brief. She didn't ask any questions. Once he'd left, I stayed with her. She said, 'Feel free to go. I'm sure you're needed elsewhere. I'm fine. Really.'

She barely ate a thing the evening before the intervention. She sipped her water hesitantly, as if each sip was too precious to her. She'd folded the clothes she'd arrived in and was keeping them under the blanket. There was nothing else in her case to wear.

That evening, I couldn't shake off the feeling that so much was missing. Things were missing, people were missing. No one had accompanied her to the hospital. Even the patients she was sharing a room with didn't offer her any companionship. With their full suitcases and the prospect of visitors, they didn't want to be infected with her loneliness.

The next day, I brought Bibi's book to work. It had often comforted me when I was missing my sister. Why shouldn't this consolation be transferable? The other nurses in theatre looked like they wanted to laugh at me, but they knew the doctor wouldn't tolerate it. They exchanged glances as I opened the book and asked the patient to tell me what she could see in the pictures. I remember her attentiveness. Her composure. The nurses' eyes upon us, briefly bewildered, then turning away.

It was the first object. The beginning of the blue box. From then on, I filled it quickly and used it at every intervention. The doctor praised me for it. He himself brought things for the box, such as the deck of cards. He'd bought it on a trip somewhere. It was so beautiful – it stood out from all the other objects.

She was the only patient I used Bibi's book with. Her name was Vera. I wasn't supposed to remember her name. I wasn't supposed to remember any of the names. It stayed with me nonetheless. Four simple letters on a passport that proved she existed.

I left the book with her until she was discharged. Then I took it home with me to the nurses' halls and put it back in my wardrobe. It wasn't meant for the hospital, I thought. Its place was in this room, with me. As long as the book was in this room, Bibi was there too.

10

'Haven't you got anything else to do?' she asked me, shuffling the cards.

'My work today is you,' I said.

'Doing this?' Marianne Ellerbach looked down at the two piles she'd dealt out.

I nodded. It was absurd, playing cards with a patient during a shift. But that's what the doctor had asked me to do. An emergency had kept him in theatre overnight. The intervention that was supposed to take place this morning had been postponed until the next day. So I sat with my patient. My time was hers.

That was the power of the doctor: he could put my time at someone else's disposal. He could release me from the units that modulated a typical day in the hospital: seven minutes for the suitcases, eight minutes to change a bed, fourteen minutes for personal hygiene. God-given units, timed at first by the older nurses, who had a clock hand ticking away inside them. Until I began to grow one inside me too.

'Where do you live, anyway?' She turned over the first card. Since the previous day, when I'd told her about Bibi and her game, she'd been asking me all sorts of things. I knew this curiosity. It seized most of the patients lying in these beds. And I knew what kind of escape they were asking for. So I borrowed stories I'd heard at dinner in the nurses' halls. I borrowed the nurses' dreams. I borrowed their men. Or I invented another life for my siblings – so simple, so detached from everything that made them who they were, that I was ashamed.

'I live in a hall of residence for nurses. Not far from here.'

'With shared rooms?' There was something about her. I didn't know what it was. I felt I couldn't possibly tell her anything borrowed or invented.

'Yes.'

'I was at a boarding school for a few years. There were shared rooms there too.' So she was used to taking her home to another place. I'd thought so. She'd arranged her personal things quickly, expertly, like someone disassembling a circus tent and putting it up again.

'Did you like it?'

She shrugged. 'I suppose I did. Sometimes I found it repellent too, that closeness. Constantly being watched. A few girls went rummaging around in each other's drawers, read other people's diaries. And the hair in the showers. The little clots of blood that got caught in it.' She wrinkled her nose. 'You could never forget you had a body, because everyone... everyone had a body, all of the time.'

'Yes. That's what it's like for us too.' Always that warm smell in the toilets. Even with my eyes closed I could tell which nurses had been before me, even before I knew their names.

'Do you go into town sometimes?'

'Now and again, yes.'

'And what do you do there?'

'Errands.'

She seemed uneasy. 'You're not a nun, are you?'

'I go out too!'

'Good. Good for you.'

I didn't hanker after restaurants and dancing like the other nurses. I only rarely went with them. And then I was like everyone else. But it wasn't my world.

Marianne put down a card. A smile spread across her face. She was about to win. 'Once I knocked out my roommate's tooth.' Her eyes went back down to the table.

'Because you were in a rage.'

'We were both in a rage. I just threw a better punch.'

I tried to read her face, her eyes, her nose, the corners of her mouth, so I could work out why she was telling me this.

'Then she gave me the tooth as a farewell gift.'

'That's… bizarre.'

'She wasn't good with words.'

'And the tooth said something specific, did it?' I put down the next card without taking my eyes off her.

'Put some effort into it!' she exclaimed. She took the card from the table and pressed it back into my hand. I couldn't help laughing. That seemed to annoy her even more.

'My sister used to do that too,' I explained. 'When she knew I was letting her win.'

'But you're not letting me win. You're just losing.' She tapped the outermost card in my hand. 'Try that one.'

I did. Her anger abated.

49

'You don't need to worry about your sister,' she said. In response to her questions, I'd told her about Bibi's travels. About the semi- and near-disasters she'd already drifted into. 'She'll come back one day. Then she can be treated too.'

'She's not coming back.' I'd only recently articulated this. It still felt strange on my tongue, like a foreign body.

'Of course she's coming back. You wouldn't believe how many times I've run away.'

'No, you don't understand. She said goodbye. The way we say goodbye in our family.'

'You mean you say cheerio instead of goodbye?'

'Never part on bad terms.'

She shook her head. 'You're a strange one, Sister.'

11

My sister cried. She was never ashamed of her tears. It enraged me. I wanted to wipe her tears from her cheeks with sandpaper. Other times, I put my arms around her and held her. 'Just cry,' I'd say, and that's what she'd do, uncontrollably. She'd shake, giving off noises like an injured animal.

There was a man on our street who liked her. That wasn't unusual. Bibi drew something out of people. They smiled at Bibi. They ruffled her hair. They told her she was a very special girl.

He lived three blocks down from us, on the ground floor, with his wife and his two girls. We saw him frequently. He worked late, so he was at home in the mornings and afternoons. There was nearly always one window open. He seemed to be immune to cold, rain and wind.

The neighbours liked him. They stopped by his window for a cigarette. They passed him letters they wanted him to translate. He could speak three foreign languages.

His wife lived in a different rhythm to him. They only saw each other for a few hours a day. My mother thought that was why they got along so well and walked hand in hand down the street at weekends. No one else over the age of seventeen did that.

Once, for a joke, my sister threw fallen leaves through his open window, armfuls of them, and of course there was some dog poo in there too. But instead of giving her a good telling-off, the man laughed at her cheek and made fun of the leftover dog poo still stuck to her hand. From then on, he greeted us whenever we passed by. 'What are you up to?' he asked. 'Where are you off to?' he asked.

'Idiot,' my sister said. 'Does he think his daughters are the only ones who go to school?' She waved without smiling.

He loved her for that. 'There's nothing like a stern face, is there, Bibi?' he said, pulling down the corners of his mouth as if to prove it.

My sister clenched her fists. 'Bibiana,' she protested. 'My name's Bibiana.'

'But if you like someone, he can call you Bibi, don't you think?'

'But I don't like you.'

He laughed again.

Every now and then, when we were playing in the street at weekends, the man would appear. He'd walk by, stop, smoke a cigarette, then wave his stupid wave. He bothered me. I knew he wasn't interested in me, and in any case he wasn't doing anything wrong. He'd just stand there, watching us and smiling.

I wanted to complain about him, but somehow I didn't know who to complain to. If I complained directly to him, he was bound to invite us into his flat to talk it over.

Or he would complain to our parents in return, and we would likely be grounded. The neighbours were out of the question, too. They held him in high esteem but thought little of us children: we were always imagining things. Bibi wanted to be someone special – and she was, but not in any way she could benefit from. She understood this, even though she couldn't put it into words.

More and more often, she wanted to take detours. We had to run half the way to get to school on time. Wilm only did this with us twice. 'Stop acting like that,' he rebuked his sister. 'Why can't you behave normally? What's going on?'

She tried to explain it to him.

'Has he offended you?'

'No.'

'Has he offended anyone else?'

'No.'

'Has he said something stupid?'

'No.'

'Has he touched you?'

'No.'

'Well then…'

'Well then what?'

'Well then, I don't get it.'

'Neither do I!'

'So just stop.'

'Stop what?'

'Acting like that. I've already told you.'

One day, she cut off her hair. She woke me in the middle of the night to show me what she'd done. 'Look,' she said, but at first I couldn't see anything in the dark. She took my hand and ran it through her short hair.

'So what do you think? Will he leave me alone now?'

Anger. I saw the anger Bibi would provoke with her new hairstyle. I saw the hair that must be lying all over the bathroom, the hair we'd find days, weeks later in the most impossible nooks and crannies. How should we explain it? Could we react at the right moment to stop things taking a turn? Should we say it was only hair? That's what it was, after all. Would we be able to sleep knowing full well the morning would begin with rage? Father would kick Bibi first, then me, then Wilm. I was tired. I didn't want this. I was tired of being spoken to because of Bibi, being asked where I was going because of Bibi, being kicked and shoved because of Bibi.

I slapped her in the face. I hit her with the palm of my hand. 'Because of you!' I cried, not even noticing how loud I was. She didn't run for cover. She didn't even duck down. 'Because of you, you bitch!' Bitch – that's what she was when we were furious with her. That's what my father screamed, that's what my mother screamed. That's even what people who liked her said sometimes. Their liking could turn into contempt. And sometimes from one minute to the next.

Bibi understood. She didn't say please; she didn't say sorry. Only her siblings said those words. Only we begged, only we tried to hide, only we hoped he would beat one of the others; take Bibi, take Wilm, not me.

She cried. I could hear her afterwards as I gathered up the hair off the toilet. It was everywhere. Everything was always a mess because of her. Now she was sobbing, gasping for breath, and soon the whole block would be awake. All because of her.

12

'No.' She gathered up the cards and shuffled them again. Just one word. No request, no negotiation. She was an Ellerbach: she called the shots. Maybe not at home, not with her brothers, and certainly not with her father. But here, there was only her and me.

'You must sleep,' I said, adding, to be on the safe side, 'the doctor says so.'

'Then you sleep here too.'

I'd already tried to leave twice. After the fifth round, I said I had to go to bed; she just shook her head, shuffled the cards and dealt them out.

I'd been in the hospital for sixteen hours. I'd spent the entire morning playing cards. Later on, I'd gone about my other duties. But I still had to check on Marianne every hour. I had to make sure she wasn't losing her nerve after all. Delays carried this risk.

She was sweating. Her body knew what lay before it. Beads on her brow, under her chin, on her neck – fever was her body's best defence. Soon, someone would arrive with a sedative for the night. I was waiting for this. Sleep would calm the body. If you're asleep, say the sedatives, you're not in danger.

I'd won the previous round. The more tired I got, the better I seemed to play. My win stirred her ambition. But I couldn't put down a bad card intentionally. She would have noticed that straight away.

'Do you like your room-mate?' she asked.

'Yes.' Sudden warmth flooded my body at the thought of Sarah. My cheeks flushed. She couldn't see it. The only thing illuminated by the light was the table where our cards lay. But maybe she could sense it, the warmth under my skin. And maybe she knew what it meant.

'I liked mine, too.'

'Really?'

'You might not believe me. Like I said, she was terribly clumsy with words. She hadn't a clue how to... manipulate anyone. Insult them. How to get under a person's skin without touching them.'

Unlike you, I thought.

'And she put up with me. She should have got a medal for that.'

'I'm sure—'

'No.' She shook her head. 'I know what I'm like.'

She said it with an astounding certainty. And what about me? I knew who I was, too. Especially when wearing this uniform. I could rely on myself. It was different when I took it off. That's when other laws prevailed.

'Too warm.' She wiped her hand across her brow. 'It's far too warm in here.' She put down her cards, pulled back the blanket and stood up. Her feet held her there for a second, but then the dizziness struck. She reached out with her hand, trying to get purchase on something, and

I leaped up, grabbed her under the armpits and helped her stay on her feet.

'I want to open the window.'

I led her round the bed. I held her weight in my arms. Everything about her was taut, like a spring. When she rattled the window catch, I placed my hand on hers and showed her that to turn it she needed to push first, then pull.

Her fingers moved through the cool night air. She drew figures in the dark. She was standing so close to me, I could feel her heartbeat, detect her stale scent, smell the fear smouldering somewhere beneath it.

She twitched slightly. I pictured her wresting free from my grasp, climbing up on the window ledge and jumping. I gasped in horror.

'What's wrong with you?' she asked.

'Nothing.' I shook off the image. 'Let's play on.'

She nodded.

She'd only put down one card when the door opened and the nurse came in with the sedative for the night.

'Hurry up,' Marianne instructed her, 'I want to finish this round.' The nurse gave me a look. I was used to it. Some understood the blue box and the time I spent with patients. Some didn't. Some, like the nurse standing before us now, hated every minute the doctor gave me. He had no business interfering in our work. He shouldn't be letting a nurse play cards. That kind of thing only led to mischief.

'All done. Goodnight.' The nurse left. I waited to see what my patient would do next. She picked up the cards again briefly. The concentration in her eyes began to dissolve. Soon, she'd fall asleep. Soon, I'd stand up and go, leaving the room and its smell behind for the night.

'If it won't hurt,' she said, the energy draining from her voice, 'what will it be like? Everyone's telling me I won't feel anything, but...' She placed the cards back on the table.

'You don't need to be afraid.'

'I'm not afraid.' She closed her eyes. 'Tomorrow, I'll disappear.'

'Your rage will disappear,' I corrected her.

'Yes.' Her hand felt around for something on the blanket. I wondered what it was. I was about to get up and go over to her things, when she found my fingers and held on to them. 'My rage will disappear.'

Then she fell asleep.

13

I woke up at her bedside. Later, I couldn't work out how this had happened. I remembered her holding my hand. I'd stayed with her. It was only supposed to be for a few minutes. Exhaustion must have overwhelmed me. It took me a moment to work out where I was, and for this to register in my stiff hands and feet. Never before had I fallen asleep at a patient's bedside. That wasn't something a nurse did.

She had her eyes open. She was facing me, looking at me. On the table between us lay the cards, untouched since the previous evening. Outside, it was still dark.

'How do you feel?' I asked. My voice sounded husky from sleep.

She blinked. I watched her closely. She was calm, not sweating. Her breathing was regular. I felt her pulse. So the sedative was working. I had no idea why she wasn't asleep.

A few strands of hair fell over my face. As I swept them behind my ear, I realized my hair was down. I reached back with my hand and felt for the knot I tied every morning and had still had in when I fell asleep a few hours ago. I couldn't find it. My hair was a mess, as if someone had been pulling at it determinedly.

Something in my stomach gave a thud. Then the nausea rose within me.

Count, I told myself. That's what I'd been taught. *Count, put your hand on your chest, feel your heart beating beneath it, and keep breathing, breathe through the nausea.* I forced myself to think of my feet. They were carrying me. They'd never let me down.

She watched me doing all this. She lay in her bed and watched me. There was no expression in her eyes. No response to what was happening.

As the nausea slowly subsided, she stirred. She turned her whole body towards me. 'Please,' she said quietly.

I shook my head. *Don't make any requests of me.*

'Describe it to me.'

'What?'

'What they're putting to sleep. My father said… it's like a tumour. It's growing. It's diseased and—'

'You need to get some rest.'

'Is that right?'

'Yes, that's right.' If that's what she wanted to think, then that's how it was. A tumour – after all, that was something to be afraid of. More than the intervention. 'One day, it could make you blind. Deaf. It could rob you of language.' *Until you're one of those hopeless creatures who don't know their own name any more. You'll be forgotten. People will stop visiting you. They won't give you a second more of their time than necessary.* 'Is that what you want, Frau Ellerbach?'

She breathed in. She held her breath. 'Marianne,' she said eventually, breathing the air out. 'My name is Marianne. I want you to call me Marianne.'

61

SARAH

1

Our room was four by four metres. It faced the street. In the distance, you could see the town with its single high-rise, the sky reflected in its smooth facade.

I'd spent the past seven years living in a first-floor room without a view, right next to the staircase. My room-mate had mostly kept to herself. She'd never crossed the invisible boundary between our beds. In the evenings, we'd sit together in the dining hall, united by the silent desire to slip the more talkative nurses a sedative.

She'd gone off to get married, leaving her life in these halls behind like an old skin. I couldn't imagine staying on in our shared room without her. The management understood this and offered me a move.

I packed my things, which didn't take long. On the second floor, I put my suitcase on the table, wandered around the room a little, and waited. Neither of the two beds seemed to be taken. One was by the window, the other closer to the door. The empty wardrobe was divided down the middle. No one had put up anything on the walls. Whoever would be living here with me hadn't arrived yet.

This room was brighter than the last one, and wasn't right next to the staircase with its constant pounding of feet. And the view, that reflective facade in the distance, kept drawing my eye.

'You want the window?' A face had appeared in the doorway.

'Yes,' I replied immediately, before adding, 'if you don't mind.'

My new room-mate looked me over, blinked a few times. No smile, but her eyes were warm. 'Okay then. You take the one by the window. I work nights – it'd be wasted on me.'

After that, I didn't see her for several weeks. She was the creases in her sloppily made bed. She was the books on her bedside table, their dog ears progressing at pace. She was the frizzy black hairs left on her pillow, and on her hairbrush.

I picked up her name in the corridor: Sarah.

2

I waited for her. Sometimes I lay in bed in our room and waited for her.

I'd always tried to bundle together my days off to give me enough time to travel home. This didn't always work out. Sometimes I had the odd day left over – not enough to make the trip.

Once I began sharing a room with Sarah, I stayed in bed longer than usual on these days. I wanted to see her, exchange a glance, a few words. I wanted to know she really existed, the woman who lived in this room without being here. The more time that passed after our first encounter, the more I seemed justified in doubting it had happened at all.

The first few times, I waited in vain. My hunger and full bladder eventually forced me out of bed. Even later, when I returned from my errands, I still couldn't find any trace of her. Was she leading a double life somewhere else? Or was she avoiding this room, and me in it? The suspicion lingered like bile at the back of my throat.

I often thought about her – that's what it's like with ghosts. I soaked up everything the nurses said about her:

she'd trained at another hospital, north of here; her ward was on the third floor. It was where babies were born. It was also where they treated the women who'd tried to prevent precisely that. Sarah was one of the eleven nurses who only worked nights. Who only wanted to work nights.

Maybe she was like us. Maybe she only felt that end-of-shift exhaustion once she'd undressed in the changing room and seen the marks the day had left on her body. The red lines where her uniform had cut into her skin. The plexus of protruding veins weaving across her arms and hands. Feet she could barely squeeze back into her shoes.

And then, like us, rushing, turning five minutes into three, knowing full well that if she stood still even for a moment, she wouldn't make it onto her bike, or into her bed, because her weariness would soon tear a chasm between herself and all other things.

Or maybe she wasn't like us after all.

It was several weeks after we first met that I saw my new room-mate again. The door handle turned long after the comings and goings in the corridor had died down. She stepped into the room and paused. She didn't notice me.

Only for a moment was she the way I remembered her. Then, with an exhausted sigh, something seemed to fall away from her. She leaned forward slightly, folding her arms behind her back. Her eyes went down to the floor, up to the wardrobe, across the table and over to the window, travelling impassively until they landed on me. 'You're here,' she said in surprise, looking straight at me.

'Yes.'

She studied me. 'So we finally get to see each other.' She took off her coat, hung it up in the wardrobe and climbed into bed, fully clothed. She lay on her side and went on looking at me. My ears throbbed with the silence between us.

'Did you have a good night?' I asked.

'No.' She pulled the blanket up under her chin. 'But now I'm here.'

My cheeks flushed. I wanted to say something, but she closed her eyes and disappeared behind them.

She soon fell asleep, her breath like a little steam train. For a while she tossed and turned, the blanket slipping from her shoulders, her black hair gradually working its way out of the loose knot she'd tied it in. I'd have never gone to bed like that, in my clothes, with the day's dirt all over me. I wanted to give her a shake, but I just looked at her.

When I eventually got up, I went over to her bed and pulled the blanket over her shoulder. I rested my hand there, just for a moment. It didn't mean anything to me then. But the image stayed with me. And it's still there. I sit on a bench, and it's there. I make a cup of coffee, and it's there. I see a window fogging up in October. And it's there.

3

I wore my dress. The dress I always wore when I went home. In this dress, I was a daughter. I'd taken care of it, patched its holes, replaced the zip. I'd never gone anywhere in it other than to my parents' flat.

The other clothes were for a different life. For a different Meret.

As I sat on the train, heading to my parents', my fingers played with the fabric. It was the summer before we started with the interventions. The summer before Sarah, back when I knew nothing of her face, nothing of what she'd do to me.

My father had had a heart attack. They'd called me once they were sure he would live. 'Of course he'll live,' my mother said on the phone, cracks riven in her voice by the fear of the past few hours.

I was a daughter. I was sure I'd always be that. There could be no life in which I was no longer that.

'What a coincidence,' said Wilm, rubbing his hands and looking at his sister as we sat together at dinner that evening.

'What else is it supposed to be?' Bibi was tired, as we all were. She had to be. A few days earlier, she'd still been travelling. She'd set off half a year ago and this was the first time she'd come home. Two nights in her old bed, then our father had had a heart attack in front of her bedroom door.

'I always said she'd be the death of me.' That's what my father had whispered to me in the hospital, smiling, pale. He loved Bibi most when he was talking about her in her absence.

I saw his white face before me as we ate – my mother, Wilm, Bibi and I. We could hear the neighbours arguing. The food was cold. We took tiny bites, forcing it down.

'You're not the only person in the world, you know,' Wilm said. He stared at his plate again.

Bibi didn't reply. Our mother, too, acted as if she hadn't heard. She was good at that. She'd taught us all to do that. Somehow you had to get by, in this flat with its two bedrooms, with its kitchen where Wilm had slept, and where he still slept when he visited. She deserved our thanks.

'At least say you're sorry.'

Bibi had always loved her brother unconditionally. When she was little, she sometimes screamed and raged so violently that my parents locked her in the kitchen. In the kitchen with all its pots and glasses and plates. But Bibi only did damage to herself. She ran into cupboards, into the door. She whacked the table edge. She kicked the oven. She lost to every piece of furniture. Wilm comforted her later. He hugged her. He placed his hand wherever it hurt. 'What was that?' he asked. 'The table? Well, it was very nasty to you. I'll get it back for that.'

'I'm not sorry.'

When Bibi said that, my mother got up from the table. She went to the toilet; we heard the flush, then her bedroom door slamming shut. Wilm put down his fork. He took a sip from his glass, swung back his arm and threw the rest of the water in his sister's face. 'Someone should give you a good beating.'

'If you say so.'

Then he too got up from the table. He stood in front of Bibi, looking down on her. I held my breath. It was so silent. It was so silent again in this kitchen. She raised her eyes to him, returning his gaze dispassionately. That was important – you had to be empty inside if you wanted to come out unscathed.

He gave up. His eyes filled with tears as he turned away from us and left the kitchen. Because there was no room he could retreat to, the front door eventually slammed shut. For a moment, I wanted to run after him. I wanted to hug and comfort him. I wanted to tell him Bibi hadn't meant it that way, had never meant it that way.

'I'm pleased you're here,' I said.

'I'm pleased he isn't dead,' she said.

A sudden thud in the night had woken my sister. When she came out of the bedroom to see what it was, he was already lying on the floor. Our mother woke up too. She phoned for an ambulance. It hadn't been a close shave. But that's how it felt.

I reached out towards Bibi and ran my hand through her hair. She didn't resist. After dinner, we lay for a while in the double bed in the dark, both awake, both pretending to be asleep, both knowing.

'He thinks it's my fault,' she said.

'That's nonsense, Bibi.'

'My brother hates me.'

I wanted to dismiss this out of hand, but she beat me to it.

'Can you remember that evening when I ran away?'

Which of the many? I wanted to ask, but I held my tongue.

'He trapped me like an animal. Like a runaway dog! He pressed me to the floor. He said, "I hate you"!'

I remembered. I'd been there. 'You said it first,' I objected. She'd even spat in his face.

'But I didn't mean it like that. I just hated him in that moment.'

Yes, she hated with all her strength, with all her body. There was a time when she'd hated me that way too. It was an eruption that travelled right through her gut. And then it was over. There was no hatred left in her body to slowly putrefy, as it did in everyone else's.

'I'm setting off again tomorrow.'

'Where to?'

'Travelling on. There's still so much I want to see.'

'You have to visit Papa before you go.'

'Of course.' She said it without hesitation. She would only hesitate tomorrow at the door of the hospital, her backpack already over her shoulders so she could reconsider, if necessary, and leave.

'Bibi, don't you want to arrive somewhere at some point?'

'Why the rush? I'm not fifty.'

'I'm not fifty either. But it's still nice to have something solid. A place where you belong. A vocation.'

'A vocation,' she repeated, and I could hear her quiet amusement. 'You know what, on paper you might not be fifty, but deep inside you've been fifty for a long time – eighty, if we're being honest.'

I pulled her hair.

'Aaaah!' she cried, feigning panic. 'Another punishment – help! Nothing but punishment in this house!' She laughed.

For a while, we lay there in silence. Eventually, her breathing became more regular. For a second, I thought she was asleep.

'He said something else before they took him away.'

If we stave off sleep for long enough, the nightmares can't get us. Neither can the ghosts. Then we have the gift of a few more hours, hours that belong to us alone. This was a law that applied only in our room.

'He said my name: Bibi, Bibi, Bibi. Like a broken record. And then he said: I'm sorry, Bibi. Forgive me, Bibi.'

Bibi. He'd never called her that. His daughter was called Bibiana.

'And have you?'

'Yes,' she said, after a brief pause. 'I stuck to it: never part on bad terms.'

4

A shoe lay on the floor. A single shoe, overturned, like a prop in a bad play. It was the first thing I saw when I entered our room after a long shift. My cup slipped from my hand at the shock of it and smashed on the floor.

'Hello,' said the head that appeared from under the blanket. 'I'm not sure there was any need for that.'

I turned to stone. I stood there like that while Sarah studied my face and waited for me to start behaving like a human being. 'It's me,' she said after a while. She pointed to herself. 'Your room-mate. Sarah. We met a few weeks ago for... two minutes, if I remember rightly. Do you remember?'

Sarah. I repeated her name in my head. Where it had often been over the past few weeks. After that night, I was sure I'd have to get used to her absence again. I'd tried to console myself with the thought of the exciting work we were doing at the hospital. That we were looking towards a future full of hope. It was actually good to come back to this room, where I could think, alone and undisturbed, about my day and the interventions.

'I know,' I said, my voice faltering. 'Of course I know who you are.'

She pulled back the blanket. Without taking her eyes off me, she came over and knelt on the floor so she could gather up the broken shards.

'Don't!' I exclaimed.

'It's no problem,' she said. 'After all, it was me who gave you a shock.'

'Your shoe.' She was too close to me. I wanted to give her a hand, but she was too close. 'Your shoe startled me.'

She looked around, then saw it. 'I see. Sorry, but I had to throw something.'

'Yes.'

'Don't you ever just need to throw something?'

A good question. 'Sometimes I'd like to,' I admitted. Then I remembered punching my pillow instead; biting and screaming into it. I wasn't a shoe-thrower. If my despair had to come out, I let it out on my pillow. Like the little child I'd once been.

'I'll go and get something to wipe this up.' She went out of the room and I stood there, stood where I was, like a pillar of salt. That's how I'd often felt at the hospital in the beginning. I stiffened into a pillar of salt when I saw people's helplessness. I hadn't known until then how ugly helplessness could be. The older nurses would hiss down my neck. They'd snatch whatever was in my hand. Wasn't that all behind me now?

Sarah came back. Her smile washed over me as she brushed past. She wiped up the spilled liquid, then left the room again. I managed to snap myself out of it. I took a few steps over to my bed, sat down and stared at the shoe. I was confused, like in those few moments after a dream.

'You wanted a cup of tea, didn't you?' Sarah returned and opened her bedside drawer. A few little bottles clinked together as she did so. 'Or do you fancy something a bit stronger? We haven't even toasted the fact that we're room-mates now.'

'But we've only met twice.'

'That's right.' She took one of the bottles from the drawer, pulled out two schnapps glasses and filled them to the brim. She handed one to me. 'To us,' she said, raising her glass to mine.

'To us,' I said, downing the schnapps in one so I didn't spill it. The alcohol burned my throat. We sat there for a while, turning the glasses back and forth between our fingers.

'I'll be here more often from now on.' She topped us both up. 'Although more often is relative when it comes to night shifts. And what about you? Always day shifts? On the fifth floor, right?'

I nodded. She must have heard things about me. Probably others complaining: that I was no fun, that I never polished my shoes properly, that I let my sister call me at all sorts of ungodly hours and didn't even wake up when the phone rang. If you'd lived as long in the nurses' halls as I had, people only talked about you if they were complaining.

'Don't worry.' She downed her drink again. 'I'm not interested in talking about work all the time. If you listened to the others here, you'd think there was nothing else in life.'

'So, what else is there in your life?'

'Well...' She smiled, caught out. 'Mainly work.'

'Are you on the third floor?'

She nodded.

'And what's it like there?'

'It's…' She looked past me towards the window. 'I still have to get used to it.'

'Is it hard with the older nurses?'

'No, it's not that. It was just different before. Freer. I went into people's homes and helped deliver their children into the world safely. It was all… so close. Now the hospital always comes between me and the women.'

'Why were you away for so long?'

She looked at me again. 'Why do you ask so many questions?'

I fell silent.

'I'd rather you told me about yourself.'

'I like it on my ward. It's—'

'About yourself!' she exclaimed, laughing. 'Tell me about you, not this hospital!'

'Oh, right.' I couldn't think of anything else to say, so instead I added, 'We haven't seen each other for weeks.' I didn't say: *I thought you were avoiding me. We missed each other too reliably. I thought you weren't like us, you didn't sleep; one life wasn't enough for you, so you had dozens of them.*

'I know.' The smile faded from her face. 'I couldn't…' She looked at her hands. 'I didn't want to come back to this empty room. The past few months have been difficult.' She poured herself a third glass, forgetting to refill mine. 'I saved up my days off so I could go and see my mother. Sometimes… I slept in the other night nurses' rooms. But things got better. From now on, I'll be a better room-mate.'

I couldn't help thinking of the last time we'd met. She'd closed the door behind herself and something had seemed to fall away from her. Her composure. Maybe she hadn't come straight from the hospital.

She had a broken heart. Now I saw it. She closed her eyes and gulped down her third schnapps.

I didn't want to be surprised by this. Nurses met men – I knew that. When they didn't have any spare hours for it, they used their spare minutes, enticing the objects of their desire into the grounds of the halls or sneaking off into dark corners. Some nurses gave up their careers for men. They left, like my old room-mate. Even so, I believed that some of them were above this. The older nurses who lived here or shared little flats in town. Those old spinsters who read the newspaper in the evenings, prompting cries of 'I'll never turn out like them!' from the younger women. But their lives didn't seem all that bad to me.

'What happened?' It was none of my business. I wanted to know everything about it. I would sympathize, smile, say something consoling, like a good room-mate. I wouldn't be disappointed that Sarah was well-practised in matters of the heart.

'Decisions were made. For a different life.' She put down her glass. She shook her head but said nothing more about it. 'Will you read something to me?'

'Read to you?' She'd said it as if it was something we routinely did.

'Anything. Preferably not sad, though. I'm really not in the mood for that.'

I looked at her pile of books.

'No, none of those.' She knocked the books off her bedside table. 'That's all a load of depressing rubbish.'

I thought of Bibi's book. I couldn't read that. The schnapps, and the courage it would give me, were out of reach.

'I'd just like to hear a story. I don't mind what. Don't you have any books here?'

'I've got a children's book.'

'A children's book?' She climbed under the blanket again. I bit my lip. I wondered if she was going to laugh at me.

'That's exactly what I need.' She stretched out. 'Was it yours as a child?'

'It was my sister's.'

I stood up and went over to the wardrobe. I pulled out Bibi's favourite story from under my folded clothes.

'She wanted to hear it over and over again. She's five years younger than me.' My tongue loosened. 'She used to sleepwalk as a child. My sister, she... I think she was afraid of sleep. Later on, she couldn't remember walking through the flat, but she was exhausted. Maybe she knew she couldn't just lie there like everyone else and sleep. Maybe she knew she wanted to cover great distances and climb stairs, and this book here was the only thing that could bring her back. A secret weapon. Our secret weapon.'

Sarah stretched out her hand. 'Show me,' she said. While the waterfall of words resounded in my head, she ran her fingers over the old pages, along the sticky tape that held the book together.

'What's your sister's name?'

'Bibiana. Bibi. There's also Wilm, my brother.'

'There's just me and my mother at home.'

Sarah closed the book. She passed it to me and shut her eyes, folding her hands across her tummy.

'I'm ready.'

When I woke again, the open book was lying by my side. Morning awaited me. Sarah was still deep in sleep. Or had she only just fallen asleep? She was a night owl, after all. Normally she clocked off when morning came. How could I have missed out on all these hours with her?

Then I remembered – she had a broken heart. She wasn't above such a thing. Instead of disappointment, I felt intense anger towards the unknown person responsible.

I took the book and placed it on her bedside table. Then I gathered up the other books she'd knocked to the floor. I wouldn't touch the shoe. It would have to wait until I came back. Or even better, lie there forever.

I stayed by her for a moment. I still had some time. I'd have to hurry afterwards, but I wanted to look at her a little longer. Watch her breathing for a moment. Maybe even dreaming; her eyelids were flickering.

The vixen will keep you company, I wrote on a torn-off piece of paper. I bookmarked the children's story with it, then placed it back on her bedside table.

When I came home in the evening, a book was lying on my pillow. The blurb promised the story of a young man who liked to walk and contemplate the world. Next to it lay a folded note: *What people who work less do. S.*

5

Sarah had meant it. Now we coincided at least once a week in our room. But I still gave a start whenever we came face to face. Like on that day in December when she appeared in the doorway. I was packing to go home.

'When's your train?' she asked, without saying hello.

My heart gave a little leap. 'In two hours.' I was always a bit surprised when I saw her face. Because it was different to the one in my mind. It wasn't about the details. I'd got those right. In fact, I could have placed the little beauty spot under her left eye with my eyes closed. But the woman before me here wasn't the one in my head.

'Mine goes in thirty minutes.' She came in, closing the door behind her. Her bag stood on the chair, ready to go, bulging with its contents. She too would soon be a daughter again.

We were allowed to travel home to our families for Christmas every other year. The thought of it brought me no joy. I pictured the kitchen table, missing a place setting for Bibi. I recalled the silence, and the eruptions that broke the silence. In our family, nothing cried out for a fight more than a festival, when everyone was supposed to come together in peace. Only our neighbours could keep this in check. When we heard them arguing through the thin walls, we were quiet. After all, we weren't like them.

'I actually hoped I'd have to work,' said Sarah. She was sitting on the bed, talking to my back.

'Me too.'

That seemed to surprise her. 'Really?' She seemed to doubt whether I was telling the truth. And I myself began to doubt whether I was telling the truth. Maybe I just wanted to please her. She brought out this uncertainty in me.

'Do I look like the others, all walking around so cheerily?'

'You look very cheery from behind.'

I laughed. Over the past few weeks, we nurses had been gripped by a sense of urgency which sent us rushing around the hospital and the halls. But there were also a few joyful souls among us who seemed immune to the non-stop end-of-year slog. In the first few months here, those from happy homes read out letters at dinner, were always on the phone, and proudly told everyone how homesick they were. Gradually, this wore off. But the old habit returned on cue before the Christmas holidays.

'Lots of fighting?'

I nodded. I couldn't help thinking of the peace; the palpable, inexplicable peace that filled the ward over the holidays.

'We fight too, me and my mother. We fight morning, noon and night. And, in between, we perform these funny rituals. We cook together, we pray and light candles, because… I don't know why, to be honest. I never know why we do all that at Christmas.'

I threw her a glance over my shoulder. 'Because it's the earth we're made from.'

She smiled. 'It's simpler here,' she said. 'When the others are away, no one can come between me and my work.'

'Is that why you always work nights?'

'Partly, yes. I love the night.'

'I don't. It scares me.'

'It's the day that scares me.'

By now I'd packed my case, so I started rearranging everything. I pushed the toilet bag from one side to the other. I rolled my socks together, then unrolled them again. I was desperate to keep my hands busy.

Sarah shuffled her feet on the floor. She seemed nervous too, like her body was feeling just as alien and awkward in my presence as mine was in hers. 'I'd like to ask you something,' she said.

I unpacked my two cardigans again, refolded them, matched each corner precisely to the other. It was ridiculous. Soon she'd notice how ridiculous I was.

'Can I?' she urged.

I realized I'd have to say something. 'Of course.'

But she didn't ask anything. The room remained silent. So I turned to her. She'd lowered her head. She's about to tell me she's going, I thought. Like my old room-mate, she'll tell me she's leaving for a new life. And I've got no way of persuading her not to.

'Will you stay here with me?' She said it so quietly, I almost didn't catch it. 'Shall we stay here?' she repeated when I didn't respond, this time louder. 'We'll unpack our things. We'll call home and say we have to work.'

Impossible. What she was suggesting was impossible. She was asking me to let the train leave without me on it, and the next one, and the one after that, until no more trains were running. She was asking me to listen to others setting off to see their families or leaving for work, one after the other, until the entire house was empty.

We'd be the only ones who wouldn't have to go any-where. No one would be waiting for us. We'd have nothing we needed to do.

'We can't,' I said.

'Okay.' She came over to me, opened the wardrobe and pulled her coat off the hanger. 'You're right.' She slipped it on. 'It was a stupid idea, wasn't it? After all, we have our...' She was looking for the right word.

'Duties?'

She picked up her bag. 'Take care, Meret. See you soon.'

'See you soon.'

And she would have gone if I hadn't burst out laughing when she turned her back on me without a final glance. It seemed so absurd to think we'd both be going home now the possibility of not doing so had suddenly presented itself. How could it be more difficult to stay than to go?

'Are you okay?' she said, furrowing her brow.

'Stay.' I gasped for air. 'Please stay.'

6

I remember those three days in such detail, as if I'd kept a record of them.

When I close my eyes, I see Sarah putting her bag back down. I hear the footsteps outside our door dwindling slowly. A final flurry of nurses setting off to see their families. Then only the building's own noises. The gurgling of its pipes in the moment of horror when I realize what we've done.

I went down to the telephone and called home. I told Wilm, who answered, that there'd been an emergency at the hospital. I was relieved he'd picked up; it wouldn't have been nearly as easy to lie to my father. After that, I changed my clothes. I hung the dress intended for the days with my family back on the hanger and slipped on a different one.

Courage had made us hungry. Together, we investigated what the larder had to offer. No one was there to cook for the nurses over the holidays, so we peeled and chopped vegetables, washed lentils, groped around in the dark corner behind the door for the bacon hidden there for special occasions. The radio freed us from awkward silences. We laughed as it churned out the old classics.

The nurses working nights stopped by and offered to help us. They laid the table and set out some candles. None of them knew we were off duty, so over dinner we joined in their complaints about the imminent shift. 'Leave it all to us,' I said, when we stood up after coffee. I took the dishes out of their hands. 'Leave it, I said!' Stunned by my stern tone, they did as they were told.

I washed the dishes in the kitchen. Sarah dried them and put everything away. Through the two windows above the sink we saw the nurses outside getting on their bikes and setting off.

When we were done, I switched off the light. Sarah turned off the radio. We stayed a few more moments in the dark kitchen.

I remember her suggesting we take a walk.

'Those straggly little bushes in the dining room are all so miserable. Shall we go and see some proper Christmas trees?'

The wood on Christmas Eve.

Needles cracking underfoot.

The dark building receiving us on our return.

I remember the cold, the radiators clanging in vain.

'Are you freezing?' She stood up, went to the wardrobe and pulled out her coat.

The weight of the wool when she placed it around my shoulders. Her garment against my skin. Her scent, enveloping me.

Then hunger came. Quietly and suddenly.

I remember two moons. One in the sky and one on the

reflective facade of the high-rise. Only briefly, when the clouds exposed it in the middle of the night.

'Look,' I said.

She was already asleep.

I was the first to wake. I looked at her. She opened her eyes as if I had woken her with my gaze.

We crept out from under our blankets. Our feet felt for our slippers, hitting the cold floor. Only I winced.

She followed me to the toilets. She washed her face while I relieved myself. I placed my two splayed palms on the wall of the cubicle. My heart was thumping.

Our eyes met in the mirror as we brushed our teeth. She was left-handed. How had I not noticed that before? I looked away quickly.

Sarah only went into the cubicle once I'd left the toilets. I nearly protested. It wasn't fair that she got to pee in privacy.

She came into the room as I was slipping off my nightdress. She did the same. She stood unclothed in my peripheral vision. She pulled her stockings up her legs. She waited until I'd taken one of my dresses out of the wardrobe, then she took hers.

I held the fabric between my hands. I went back to the wardrobe. The dress I'd put back yesterday was hanging there. The dress I was a daughter in, only ever a daughter. A dress with an embroidered collar. I never wore it here in the halls, except on the days I was travelling home. I took it out and hung the other back up.

'Merry Christmas,' she whispered. She smiled. She too

had put on her best dress. The buttons ran all the way down from her neck to her knees.

There were only two older nurses sitting in the dining room at breakfast, reading newspapers. They looked up briefly, gave us a nod, then went back to reading. *It's fine*, I told myself. *We're not doing anything illegal.*

We each took a piece of cake someone must have baked early that morning. We filled our cups with coffee and sat down at one of the tables. We ate in silence.

Now the next three days opened up endlessly before me. Hours like sand on the beach, filled with nothing but us. I looked at her. She appeared so unconcerned. I envied her.

'So, what now?' I asked, after we'd brought our plates and cups into the kitchen.

'Come on. I have an idea.'

We fetched our coats.

'Wait,' she said, as I was about to go out of the door. 'We can't turn up looking like this.' She knelt down and brushed her shoes. She stamped her feet a few times, and pine needles from our evening walk fell from her soles onto the doormat. She passed me the brush and waited patiently while I brushed off weeks and weeks of dirt. 'Now we're all set.'

She rode on ahead. I followed her, cycling through the almost empty streets, past the low-roofed terraces and a house with a green door, where we turned off towards town. There were few people out and about.

We stopped at the church on the marketplace.

'We're here. Shall we go in?'

My eyes came to rest on a bench near the entrance. 'No.'
'I prefer it outside too.'

We got off our bikes. People streamed past us into the service. We sat down and watched the latecomers hurrying in. The last one closed the heavy door behind him.

For a few seconds, all we could hear was the wind. Then the sermon began. We listened to the muted voices. The congregation singing. Sarah had closed her eyes.

There was a choir on the street where I had grown up, and I thought about this as we sat on the bench. I didn't know exactly where the choir was, or why it was there. All I knew was that I heard it sometimes in our bedroom. I heard it in the late evening by the open window. It felt like it was coming from another world, and I fell asleep to its song.

We lay on our beds and marvelled at the empty hours. We kept the older nurses company in the kitchen. They read out a crime novel after dinner, and we laughed with them at the outrageous twists. We crept around the house aimlessly.

We went through all the items in the small room by the pigeonholes where the nurses deposited things they no longer had any use for. Ashtrays marking the beginning and end of a vice. Unused pens and paper. A pretty cardigan and a new pair of shoes from one of the nurses who came from a well-off family and had no need for them. Sarah took the cardigan. I took a drawing of an old woman peeling apples. Back in my room, I hung the picture above my bedside table.

We planned the next meal. We showered with our backs to one another, longer and more luxuriously than we ever had before. I held my head under the streaming water for several minutes. She turned the water to cold and shrieked. 'Your turn!' she yelled across the tiled room. I reached for the tap and turned it right round to the left. The ice-cold water poured over me, stopping my breath. Afterwards, I dried myself off, wheezing. I felt her eyes on me briefly. Then she looked away again.

7

Cycle to the house with the green door. I'll be waiting for you there at 7.30 p.m.

She'd pushed the folded note into my locker. I found it as I was getting ready to go home.

We would tell each other which days we had free; we'd promised each other this on the day after Christmas, before we fell asleep. It had been her suggestion. After that, whenever we parted after spending a few hours together, we said, 'See you Tuesday.' 'See you Saturday.' 'See you in ten days.' Those were fleeting hours. I had her with me, I blinked, and she was gone again.

I'll be waiting for you at 7.30 p.m. I stared at her words. Then I remembered myself and reached for my watch. Twenty past seven.

I'd only ever moved that fast when I'd seen the abyss during a shift. I tucked her note into my stocking, threw off my uniform, slipped on my dress, cardigan and coat and stepped into my shoes. I thrust open the door, shoving it into some nurses coming the other way, apologized in haste but didn't stop. Then I raced off, raced through the wood, trusting my hands to brake at the right time, trusting my bike to hold steady. I managed, of course. I'd known this path like the back of my hand for a long time.

When I saw her outline at the traffic lights my stomach filled with butterflies. She was leaning on her saddle, watching me. 'There you are,' she said. Again, she didn't smile. She never smiled when we greeted each other. It was as if she needed a few minutes in my company before this impulse came over her.

'I'm sorry,' I gasped.

She placed her hand on mine. 'Just breathe.'

I noticed my knees trembling. My vision clouded. I thought I was about to faint.

'Here.' She gave me a bottle of water. I drank until my body calmed down. 'There's somewhere I'd like to show you. It's not far. Will you come?'

Now she was smiling. Smiling in the darkness, as if she knew that I would go anywhere with her, that I didn't have a choice.

As we cycled through the streets, I took in the nocturnal sights. There were a few people around, their shoes clip-clopping on the paving stones, their voices rising up the walls of the houses, relaxed and merry. I hoped Sarah didn't want to take me somewhere indoors. The light would mercilessly show up my haste, my exhaustion, the day clinging to every part of my body.

We stopped outside a restaurant. I'd been there before. I'd huddled round a table with the nurses one night, drinking cheap alcohol. I was so relieved when we'd finally left and I could ride back through the night to the halls. I'd loved my old room-mate because she gave me privacy; she never crossed the invisible boundary between our beds, she didn't need entertainment, and in all those years her heart was only broken twice. Unlike the others, whose hearts broke constantly, organs prone to fault, barely patched up before the next person tore them apart again.

'Are you coming?' Sarah placed her hand on my shoulder and I felt a hole in my stomach, a void that tried to withstand her touch.

I let her pull me inside. We were given a table.

Sarah waited until the waiter had gone away, then whispered, 'Leave your coat on. Stand up.' She hooked her arm in mine, led me to the toilets and pushed open the door to the emergency exit. 'Up to the top,' she said, and I obeyed without question, beginning to think I was dreaming and was still lying asleep in the changing room. I was only dream-walking up this staircase, holding on to its bare walls because the handrail was coming loose, with her at my back.

We came out into the open air.

'Look,' she said. She gently swivelled me around and pointed to the building opposite. It rose many storeys above us, projecting into the sky, the stars reflected in its smooth facade. 'Do you recognize it?'

She'd brought some bread with her, a bottle of wine and two glasses. We drank in silence while the clouds passed across the facade, briefly exposing the moon then swallowing it again. It was cold on the roof. The cold whistled through the air, found every bit of exposed skin and crept through our clothes.

'Where do you come from?' I asked eventually, when I could barely feel my fingers any more. There were no photos in our room to give me any kind of clue. I hadn't hung anything up either, apart from my new drawing. The photo of me and my family was stowed away in my drawer. Until now, almost all my questions had come to nothing.

'My mother was forty-eight when I was born,' she said. 'Just imagine. She was on her own nearly all her life. She would have preferred to stay that way.'

'That's not true.'

'Of course it's true.' She refilled our wine glasses. 'But is it bad? I don't think so.'

Sarah moved up a bit. Not for her own sake, I thought, because she was immune to the cold. She'd placed her coat around my shoulders on Christmas Eve when she was only wearing her nightdress. She walked around our room barefoot. While sleeping, she wound herself out of the blanket. I could see her bare skin. If I covered her up, she broke free again.

'I'm descended from ghosts,' she said, running her hands through her hair. 'My grandparents, my aunts – I didn't know any of them. They all died before I was born. And as for my father... there's no photo of him. I have my mother's hair and mouth, but I don't know what I got from my father and what God happened to come up with for me...' She shrugged. 'I know he was a tourist. He must have ended up in our neighbourhood by accident. I'd be amazed if not. There's nowhere less worth seeing than our neighbourhood. He stayed with my mother for ten days.

And I was the result. My mother always said it was a miracle.'

'That's nice.'

'She didn't mean she got lucky.'

'Do you know his name?'

'Maurice.' She showed me her empty palm. 'See? There's almost nothing I can love him for.'

'There's you, though.' I wanted to put my hand on hers. There were only a few centimetres between us for me to bridge. 'Can't you love him for that?'

She smiled, shoving her hand back in her pocket. 'And what about you?'

'I've already told you lots.'

'You told me your sister went away?'

'Yes, after my father had his heart attack.'

'A strange time to leave.'

'She'll come back, of course. Eventually. When she's seen enough of the world.'

'That can't be possible.' Sarah ran her tongue over her lips. 'To have ever seen enough of the world.'

On the way home, she slammed on her brakes. She got off her bike and went over to take a closer look at a stool someone had left outside a house. *Please take*, said the note stuck to it. 'Look at this!' she exclaimed. 'It's for us!'

I couldn't stop her. First of all, she tried to fasten the stool to the bike; then she carried it on her shoulder, convinced it belonged in our room and that a plant needed to stand on top of it, like in a proper home.

'So, who broke your heart?' I asked once we were back in our room. We were sitting on our beds, still in our clothes. There was a rush of blood to my ears. It felt like I could ask her anything.

She looked down into her tea. She said nothing in response, and the seconds began to stretch out. Cold spread through my stomach.

'It's constantly being broken,' Sarah said eventually. 'I cycle to the hospital, knowing that when I get home I'll have to piece it back together. Not always. There are days when everything suddenly makes sense, but... you know how it is. How they are towards the patients.'

'Not all of them.' I was a bit loud. 'Not all of them are like that,' I added more softly.

'You mean the doctor on your ward?' She put down her cup. 'You mean you?'

Her tone irritated me. I said nothing else.

She could tell straight away. 'Sorry,' she said quietly. 'I didn't want our evening to end like this.'

Sarah stood up, took off her coat, hung it in the wardrobe and slipped off the rest of her clothes behind the half-open door. Button by button, the contours of her body emerged. Her left shoulder. Her left breast. Her ribcage. Her hip bones. The line beneath, pointing down between her legs.

She looked over at me. I'd been caught, but I couldn't look away. And her eyes weren't asking me why either. They were studying me. They went right through me.

'I wanted to share a moment with her in a room. We were only ever together in public. There were a few minutes here, an hour or so there. I felt like a dog. I'm only given enough food to survive. But my hunger…' She pulled her nightdress over her head. 'My hunger never goes away.'

She closed the wardrobe and crawled into bed under her blanket. 'And what about you?' she asked. 'Who broke your heart?'

'No one. At most, my sister when she left.'

'But she'll come back.'

I nodded. 'She'll come back.'

8

A few days later, I had some time off. I woke when Sarah came into the room after her shift. We wanted to use the daylight hours to sand down the stool. We'd agreed this when we'd last seen each other.

'I'll just lie down for a few minutes,' she said by way of greeting, 'then I'll be ready.' She threw her coat over the back of the chair. Still in her clothes, she climbed under the blanket and fell asleep straight away.

So I spent the day in her sleeping company. I knew I shouldn't start on the stool without her. I read, washed my clothes, took a shower, then lay in bed listening to her breathing.

She woke as dusk was falling, reproaching me only half-heartedly for not waking her sooner. I brought her a coffee and a few slices of bread. We went looking for sandpaper, primer and paint in the cellar, then went outside and stood with the stool in the setting winter sun.

'It was a long night,' she said. 'I wish I could have stayed awake and spent the day with you.'

My cheeks flushed.

'Sometimes I hate them.' She reached into her coat pocket, took out a packet of cigarettes and offered me one.

I shook my head. I picked up the sandpaper and got to work.

'The patients. Sometimes I hate them. With every fibre of my being. I could kill them all.'

The glowing match lit up her face. She held it between her fingers, and I thought: she's about to set fire to the stool; it's about to go up in flames in my hands.

'I hate the way they're treated.' She lit her cigarette and blew out the match. 'I think it's their own fault – why are they so stupid, anyway? I hate the fact they're in pain, and that you can see it. Then I realize how unfair I'm being, and I hate myself, and I want to kill myself.'

I said nothing. There it was, that familiar nausea between my ribs. Not like at other times, when I had to breathe through it and count. But it was there.

'Don't you ever feel that?'

'No.'

She furrowed her brow. Then another pause, because she didn't believe me. I recalled the despair. That pitch-black despair always lurking on the ward, waiting for hopelessness to set in.

'It can be hard,' I admitted, 'but hatred… It's good work. It does so much…' *Good*, I wanted to say. I couldn't get the word out. She nodded.

Outside in the courtyard, the two of us alone together, I wanted to tell her everything in detail. I wanted to tell her about the young man who, thanks to the intervention two days ago, had been cured of his destructive rage and could do no more damage. I wanted to tell her about the strength I'd needed to get him through the intervention. *Hold on to me. I'll make sure you get through this.*

But something about her stopped me. A scepticism in her eyes whenever we talked about the hospital. All the certainty and strength my work gave me shrank to a vague pretension in her presence. So I didn't talk about it much. If I mentioned the older nurses, the patients, the intervention, I'd see her sceptical expression and change the subject. She did the same. She'd start telling me something, only to break off mid-sentence, saying that that was enough, that we'd said we wouldn't talk about it, that it just tainted everything, and had I seen the story in the paper today about the fire?

She took a last drag, then stamped out the cigarette on the floor.

'Your family home.' I blew some dust off the stool. It swirled in the air and landed on her coat. She didn't brush it off. 'What was it like?'

'What was it like?' *Haven't I told you enough?* her eyes seemed to be saying.

There was her and her mother. There was a neighbour who sometimes came over for a cup of tea and then stayed for days. There was the rusty old car her mother picked her up from the station in when she went home. The passenger door would spring open without even a 'hello', and she'd be met by the first torrent of *Justlooktheweather, Whyareyoustandingbackhere, Whatonearthdoyoulooklike.*

Her house was on a large plot of land. There was so much sky, it tired you out. There were photos of great-aunts, grandparents, all of them gone before Sarah was born.

The rooms in her house were damp. Like the cellar in the nurses' hall, where we'd rummaged through the rubbish, looking for sandpaper. Like in the hospital, in the changing rooms. 'Sometimes I stand in that hospital,' said Sarah, 'and suddenly' – she snapped her fingers – 'I feel like I'm back at my mother's. As if she and I are breathing the same air. Because it smells exactly the same. Because I have the same feeling here inside.' She placed her hand on her stomach.

'That's happened to me before too.'

'Really?'

I shoved her shoulder, harder than I'd intended. 'Don't you believe me?' I cried. She had to step back to keep her balance. I saw this, and all my audacity ebbed from me. 'Sorry,' I murmured, lowering my head.

She came towards me, took hold of my chin and pushed it upwards. 'I'm not made of glass,' she said.

In that moment, I wanted to sink the weight of my head into her hand. I wanted to close my eyes and rest there.

We carried the stool from one corner of our room to another and back again. We couldn't seem to find the right place for it. Eventually we stood it in the middle of the room. 'Our lighthouse,' said Sarah, putting a candle on it.

Now, with this unnecessary piece of furniture standing in it, the room seemed stark.

'Can I see the postcards from your sister?'

I nodded. I took the little pile from the drawer and showed it to her.

She whistled appreciatively through her teeth. 'We should pin them up,' she said. 'Your sister's travelling all over the world.'

'Not exactly.' I turned over a postcard and began reading it out: 'Dear Meret... I'm still working on the farm, and for two weeks now the sky has looked like it's about to drop a bucket of divine shit all over... which is why I'm sending you this postcard from the South of France...'

'There's no need to cry,' said Sarah.

'I'm not crying.'

I wasn't my sister. I didn't sit in front of others, crying shamelessly, as if I were proud of my pain.

'I'm going to buy a houseplant,' I said, 'for the stool. From the florist's at the station.'

'No.' She put her hand on mine. 'We'll do that together. You and me. Agreed?'

Why wouldn't I agree?

9

She was kneeling by her bed, her elbows propped on the mattress, resting her forehead on her folded hands.

That's how I found her in the semi-darkness. The snow lying outside cast a cold light into the room. It took a moment for me to make out her shape. But I knew she was there. We knew each other well enough now to sense the other's presence before entering the room.

The door was slightly ajar. I opened it a little, gently. It was already late; night had fallen.

I blinked. I wasn't sure I was seeing right. She was whispering, her eyes closed. She didn't notice me.

Closing the door quietly, I went downstairs. I sat alone at one of the long tables and ate my dinner. I'd been a witness to something intimate, more intimate than a naked body, more intimate than tears.

Lost in confusion, I listened to the noises of the house. The wooden beams creaking in the cold, the whooshing in the walls – the unmistakable sound of nocturnal visits to the toilet. Eventually her footsteps on the stairs too. She stopped in the doorway. 'Come into the warmth,' she said.

I was beyond tired. I didn't want to lie down. I knew that if I did, I'd spend the night with my thoughts. 'I'm going out again.'

'It's freezing out there.'

Ice crystals were branching across the windows. The last throes of winter. It was the end of March.

'Come with me,' I said.

Taking our bikes, we rode to the end of the asphalt road. Usually the wood greeted its visitors like a wall of black, but now the snow gave it contours, made it softer, almost inviting. We parked the bikes and took the pathway we'd gone down on Christmas Eve, knowing it would bring us back again.

We were silent. The snow had spread its blanket over every sound. All we could hear was the crunch of our feet on the ground, our breath, and every now and then something snapping in the thicket.

Many of the nurses were afraid of the wood. When it was dark and they were cycling alone, they took a long detour to avoid it. There were stories, and they were all frightening in their own way. I wasn't afraid of the wood. I trusted in the path I travelled, day in and day out. I was sure this familiarity protected me.

Sarah went on ahead. She could never stay beside me for long when we were on the move. I knew her back so well by now. I knew the way it tilted slightly on the bike. I knew its upright posture when she walked, and the pride she took in it – I knew how she defended it against exhaustion.

It started snowing again. At first I thought it was an illusion, just snow being scattered from a tree by a gust of wind. But then the flakes came more heavily. They fell on the ground, the trees and the bushes. On Sarah's hair. She stretched out her hand and caught a few.

I took a deep breath and held it in. I didn't want to see its frozen clouds. I wanted to see that hair, and the snow slowly turning it into a landscape.

When we got back from the wood to our room, the window was wide open. Neither of us could remember opening it. Snow lay on the floor. 'No!' I cried. Now we'd freeze all night long. Sarah laughed at how hurriedly we'd left.

I got changed quickly and climbed into bed. I was still warm from the journey, but that didn't last long. The sweat cooled on my skin. I curled up, making myself as small as possible, arms wrapped round my knees to keep in the rest of the warmth. I looked at Sarah. She was freezing like me, a shivering little ball in her bed. She wasn't immune.

'Come and lie with me,' Sarah said eventually.

It wasn't unheard of. Nurses often slept in the same bed. To warm each other up, to comfort each other, to deaden the hopelessness. That's what I told myself as I accepted her invitation. She put her arm around me; I felt her in my back, in my neck, in my hair. She was shivering, but her body was warm. She took my hand. I kissed her knuckles. Her wrist. Her forearm, following the arteries running down it.

10

I was convinced it wasn't me. It wasn't me who'd stripped naked so her hands could be with my body. It wasn't me who'd kissed her ears in this ice-cold room, who'd surrendered my tongue to hers, offered up my hair and neck when she reached for them. It wasn't me who'd run my fingers between her thighs, or pushed them apart so I could touch her. It wasn't me who'd felt her body start to quiver, one hand gripping the sheet, the other pulling me towards her until my forehead was touching hers.

It wasn't me who'd stopped at some point, opened my eyes and exchanged this astounded look with her. It wasn't me who, still naked and sweating, had rested my head on her shoulder and succumbed to a fast, black sleep, like unconsciousness. It wasn't me, because, well, how could it have been?

Me – the person who woke in the middle of the night, peeled herself, bewildered, off this other body, stepped into her shoes, hurried to the toilet, slapped cold water on her face and said to herself in the mirror: that must have been someone else. And then stumbled back into the room and saw Sarah sleeping soundly, perhaps even contentedly, perhaps even dreaming sweet dreams. I was the person who let the remains of this night turn into morning and started her day, a day barely distinguishable from any other.

That was the story with shame.

There was also one without.

I kissed her forearms.

I kissed her collarbone.

I kissed the place between her breasts.

I kissed her mouth, the mouth my eyes had lingered on so many times.

She reached for my hair. My neck. She whispered into my mouth that she was wet. That I made her wet.

I ran my fingers between her thighs and pushed them gently apart. I touched her hot wetness, felt the pull in my abdomen, and realized I was wet. That she made me wet too.

'What now?' I asked.

'Inside,' she said. 'I like it inside.'

I looked at her. I wanted to see what was happening on her face. And because there was barely any light, because we had to be quiet, only her breathing could help me find my way: not there. Or: right there.

Then I moved away from her. I wasn't close enough to my fingers. I pushed myself down her body, my head between her thighs, so I could see exactly what she looked like, even though most of her was in the shadow of my own face. I felt my way forward with my tongue. I didn't just want to smell her. I wanted to taste her.

Her body started to quiver, one hand clenching, gripping the sheet and the other groping about for me, unsure
whether to stop me and at the same time insisting I should
absolutely not stop because with each touch more and
more was falling from her and she could hardly bear it.
I carried on, pushing my fingers deeper inside her until
the quiver became a spasm and she grabbed a pillow and
placed it over her face. It barely stifled the gasp of surprise
that escaped her lips.

I followed her hand, which pulled me towards her. We
exchanged an astounded look. I let her kiss me. I watched
her trace her lips with her tongue, smiling.

'Now you,' she said.

But I didn't want to leave the moment. 'Just stay like
this with me?'

I lay naked, soaked in sweat, my head on her shoulder, and a deep, fast sleep came over this happiness, like
unconsciousness.

In the middle of the night I woke. I peeled myself,
bewildered, off her warm body. I stepped into my shoes,
hurried to the toilet and slapped cold water on my face.
I looked at myself in the mirror. The little groove between
my nose and lip, covered in fine down. The one eyelid
hanging lower than the other. I traced my fingers along
the bones that stood out under my skin: my cheeks, my
jaw, my forehead.

That was me. That's how I looked.

When I crept back into the room, she was sleeping
soundly. I could still fit perfectly into the hollow formed
by her body. Lying like that, I let the remains of the night

turn into morning. At one point, I took her hand, kissed it, and marvelled at my own smell on her fingers.

Eventually she woke up. We started the day together.

11

Sixteen square metres, two beds, a wardrobe, a table, a chair. A stool that needed a plant on it, like in a proper home.

We left things for each other. Books, chocolate, a freshly picked flower. Little notes telling each other what we'd been doing. She wrote about a stubborn bike chain, and about her mother, who'd gone to get her jacket during a phone call only to then forget about her daughter altogether. I wrote about Bibi's last postcard from Australia and about the ant colony in the toilet.

In the evenings following our first night together, I lay in bed, my eyes lingering on these things, feeding off the snippets of daily life that Sarah chose to share with me. They got me through the nights I was alone.

The time we spent together in this room:

Saying 'hello'. Taking off my jacket and hanging it in the wardrobe.

Attending to a few important things before turning to one another: going to the bathroom, washing the hospital off me, if not off my whole body then at least off my hands, arms and face.

Patching up my uniform, which had torn at the sleeve. Closing my eyes and going through the handover with the night nurse again so I could erase the hospital from my head too.

Eventually being interrupted by her voice: 'May I?'

'Yes.'

She came towards me, placed her hands on my cheeks and kissed me. We laughed. Our laughter cleared my head.

Trying so hard to stay awake that my temples hurt because my body was tired, because it wanted to lie with her and sleep. Protesting because I wanted to stay conscious and catch everything she said.

Sleep, sinking me like a stone.

Sounding out her past: 'Who was your first kiss?'

'A girl from my village. To thank me, because I'd given her my bike.'

Sarah came and stood behind me as I looked out of the window. She wrapped her arm round me so it lay on my collarbone, stroking my shoulder with her thumb. I could have closed my eyes and stayed like that for hours.

'She was my first time, too. It all went wrong. It was as if we couldn't tell top from bottom. But—'

'But?'

'It felt like home. Like being home.'

She leaned her head against mine.

'And you?'

'A girl from my school.'

'A girl too?'

'All the girls kissed girls back then.'

'I'm not surprised.' Her hand wandered along my arm. She clasped my hip and pulled me closer to her.

Casting off these things when our time ran out. As the alarm clock ticked away the final minutes, we detached ourselves from one another. We took off the clothes we'd been together in. We combed our hair and put it up. We left the room and slapped cold water on our faces.

We never kissed each other goodbye.

There were cool hours too. It could suddenly switch. We were sitting together when she said, 'At some point, I want to show you where I grew up. Introduce you to my mother. She's a bit like an out-of-tune piano. I think you'd get along.'

I nodded. I didn't want to leave this room. Things were simple here: one of us came home, and the other was already there. One of us closed the door, and the rules of the outside world no longer applied.

She stood up. She reached for her pillow, went to the window and shook it out. She smoothed out her sheet and blanket more than ever before. She's about to go and get the broom, I thought. And then she did. I took a deep breath. One of her characteristics: turning anger into order.

I waited until she'd finished sweeping. Until even the books were freed from their thin layer of dust.

Then she stood by the door. She wanted to leave. I would have let her. She knew that.

Sarah sat down beside me on the bed again. She opened her mouth, shook her head and moved away when I tried to put my hand on her shoulder. Slowly, very slowly, exhaustion came and drove the hardness out of her.

'She fell off her bike.'

'Who?' Her profile betrayed it without a reply.

'When it happened, we hadn't been... whatever we were... for a long time. We continued writing to each other. Phoned each other now and again. It was... always peaceful for about two minutes, then things would explode. She was impossible. Moody. Always thought she knew best. We probably wouldn't have been able to stand each other for much more than a week.'

Her broken heart. I recalled the schnapps we'd drunk to it.

'She was an addict.'

'Morphine?' It was a common addiction. People's need for opiates supplied entire towns with work and entire cemeteries with corpses, the doctor liked saying. He was so wary of these kinds of remedies that he refused any relief for his back pain, even when it was at its worst.

Sarah nodded. 'She had several courses of treatment. I don't know. I don't think I have the capacity to understand it. Or maybe I understand it all too well. I don't know.' She clutched the blanket. Dug her fingers into the fabric. 'She fell off. She was taken to hospital. The doctor there knew her. They treated her for schizophrenia. With the usual methods. Not for concussion... even though she'd hit her head on the asphalt.' She exhaled heavily. Her voice was trembling. I thought she was going to cry. She was about to cry. I really didn't want her to cry.

'Did you see her?' She said nothing, and I understood. I understood where her broken heart came from.

'I can't assume they had any bad intentions. I wish I could – that would make it easier. I think they saw something sick and wanted to treat it. And that's what they did. Until there was nothing left of her.' She closed her eyes. 'It's because of her that it's different. That I'm different.'

I sensed she'd shared something with me that lay buried deep under everything else I knew about her. I sensed it, and I felt special, and I didn't want to.

'You're proud of your work. I understand that. I am too. Despite everything.' She turned her gaze directly on me. 'But it's not that simple. Things aren't as simple as you'd sometimes like them to be.'

I nodded. You just had to leave her. I knew that by now. You just had to let her be, and then she'd start talking about something else of her own accord.

12

It was already late when we met at the house with the green door. We'd arranged to buy a houseplant. Over the past few weeks, Sarah had often looked at our stool with reproach in her eyes. 'Just let me get it on my own,' I'd say then. Our time together always seemed too brief to squander it in a place where I couldn't touch her.

'No. You and me. We'll do it together.'

We cycled to the station. There was a shop there that never closed, supplying people with flowers and plants at all hours of the day.

Sarah rode on ahead. The wind stirred her tied-back hair, the hair that lay all over our room, in the showers, in the washbasins, and got caught in the plugholes. I liked taking hold of it. When I held it, it was as if that was all my hands had been made for.

We chained our bikes together. Sarah hadn't smiled yet, or glanced over her shoulder the way she always did when we were cycling and she was racing on ahead. Since she'd told me about her friend, a piece of her had disappeared behind that familiar silence. I wasn't to ask about her. Her memories of her. Her name.

'Are you sure we'll find something here?' she said, peering into the shop from outside. She clearly hadn't seen it before. She didn't know that this was where people made a hasty stop before catching their train. They'd stare into the buckets. Try, unsuccessfully, to make up a bouquet. Call out to an assistant for help. *Excuse me*, they'd say, catching their breath, *I'm in a rush. Could you please…* and the assistants were so experienced that they didn't even need to ask what the occasion was – they could tell by the faces in front of them.

'Of course we will.' I went inside, past the buckets and two customers, to the plants at the back. The assistant nodded at me. 'Family' was what he usually muttered when I came in. I always bought flowers for my parents before getting on the train to visit them. The assistant would make up a slim, modest bouquet for me. Here and there he'd intersperse some bright flowers, evoking spring when outside there was no weather, only grey.

'Something that doesn't need too much sun,' said Sarah. She pointed to the bottom row of plants.

'The one with red in the leaves?'

'Good choice.'

She took hold of the plant and brought it to the till. The assistant looked from her to me, waited for my nod, then took our money begrudgingly.

'What's wrong with him?' she asked once we were back on the station concourse.

I explained the laws of the florist's to her. How we'd broken them by not asking for advice.

'Do you buy flowers for your family?'

'I buy them for my dad, actually. He loves flowers. But he'd never admit it.' I saw it in his eyes whenever I handed him the bouquet. A secret joy, just a flicker.

'He must be a great father if his daughter brings him flowers.'

'He's… a father.'

Sarah burst out laughing. Instead of making for the exit, she went in the other direction, to the tracks. 'Come on, we'll sit on the platform for a bit.'

There wasn't much going on. The last trains were pulling in and picking up their passengers. I wanted to go back to our room. I didn't need the outside world. Not the way she did.

'Why did your sister leave?'

'She didn't leave.'

Sarah snorted. I could sense her irritation. I was irritated myself. She had a way of exposing something within me, something that had no edges, no handles, nothing I could hold on to. It was the opposite of security, the opposite of the silent assent between our bodies as they touched one another.

'She's difficult, my sister. She doesn't care about… the fundamentals. Rules. The rules of coexistence.'

'Did you fall out sometimes at home?'

'It's a bit cramped in the flat. That's all.'

She nodded. 'My mother can be cruel too.' She scraped the floor with her foot. 'In her own way.'

'What do you mean?'

'She leaves you completely on your own. Without even leaving the room. She might be sitting at the same table, but she's just… gone.'

'Like you.'

Sarah put her hand to her chest as if she'd taken a punch. She looked down at the floor, then turned her eyes to the advertising boards. 'I always get the train from here when I go to hers,' she said.

'Mine goes from this platform too.' The train went directly to the station where Bibi had picked me up during those first few years. Bibi with my mother. My mother, whom I saw in the mirror, in the corners of my mouth, my chin, my cheeks. Who listened to my excuses when I cancelled yet another visit because since Sarah, every day off had become precious. 'Lots to do?' she'd ask down the phone, going along with the lies instead of pushing me for the real reason I was staying away. My mother, who kept saying, 'Wait until he's older. Then he'll be easier to love.'

But it wasn't that hard. It never had been. Not even during the beatings. It was only afterwards. When he stopped, and his body collapsed. This exhaustion always made him tearful. 'Forgive me… please, forgive me.' Then he wanted to hold his children in his arms. He only let them go once they'd allowed him to hold them, once they'd said, 'It's okay. It's okay.'

'It doesn't really happen any more.' I shrugged. 'We had it better than most. Only my sister… she wouldn't let him apologize afterwards. She'd scream "Get off me," "let me go," play games, provoke him. She just can't stop, she…'

I shook my head. There it was again, exposed, and I was slipping off its smooth surface. What for? If these things stayed inside us, unspoken, we were spared them when we were together.

'But it's not her fault.' Sarah looked at me. She reached out and tucked a strand of hair behind my ear. I wanted to defend myself. I wanted to explain to her that it certainly was Bibi's fault, but I was taken aback by her gesture.

She kept her hand in the air. Was she about to grab me by the throat? Put her hand on my collarbone and rest it there? But then she pulled it back again and ran her fingers over the leaves of the plant instead.

On the platform opposite, two women were running for the train. One was out in front, the other gasping for breath behind her. What if that was Sarah and me? Running with our cases because we were going away, somewhere else, like she wanted?

'Supposing we set off to your house,' I said, 'how would we get there?'

'First, we'd sleep on this bench here. Then we'd take the train at quarter to seven. We'd travel for two hours, change, then chug for another three hours through nowhere in particular. My mother would pick us up. She wouldn't introduce herself – she'd have to have a good rant first. You'd look up and the sky would seem endless, even more endless than here. You'd think to yourself, the sea will appear any moment now, but it wouldn't. Then, before you knew it, we'd be there.'

'I like the sound of that.'

She lay her head on my shoulder. 'Me too.'

MERET

1

First stop: the changing rooms. There were still a few hours to go before Marianne's intervention. I wanted to take a shower and sort out my hair. I went down the stairs behind the entrance, following the smell of damp, holding on to the banister, trying not to slip on the steps. It felt like the rain was always there, hammering on the building from outside, saturating the air in the room, creeping into the walls. Those who'd got ready before us were still there. I smelled their sweat. I felt the warmth of their bodies.

This was where, in the lost hours between morning and midnight, you'd find them, just sitting here, the nurses who'd seen the abyss. They couldn't walk away. They thought if they sat for long enough, they could leave it here, simply slip it off with their uniform.

But not today. Today I was alone. No opening and closing of lockers, no slipping off of clothes or shoes, no rolling up of stockings. We pulled them up over our knees before each shift, checking for ladders and stains. We inspected each other's faces. A mirror might lie to you. Another nurse wouldn't.

I threw my uniform into the laundry basket and stepped under the shower. I turned the water on so hot that it burned my skin. I thought about the fact that Sarah was working right now, in the hospital wing. That she was awake, like me, that her heart was beating, like mine.

She didn't exist here. Not really. Only within me. I carried her with me through these rooms. But I never met her in the corridors, never in this changing room. I made every effort to keep it this way, to keep her apart from my working life. But despite the rotas, which drew a clean separation between our shifts in the hospital, I sometimes imagined her near me, her black ponytail, a hint of her scent, her voice rippling in the air. That's when I moved on quickly. I didn't even know which locker was hers. I didn't want to know.

My hair. Combing it out. Putting it up. I looked for the little box I kept my hairgrips in. 'Here,' Sarah had said, pressing it into my hands after one of our first nights together. 'Keep them. Think of me when you use them.'

I opened the box. A black hair was tangled in one of the hairgrips. It was always there when I opened the lid. At first, it seemed like a memento, the only thing I'd managed to save from a fleeting dream. But after that, whenever I got back to our room I found Sarah there.

She was there. And right then, I believed she always would be.

Fastening the cap. Looking at myself in the mirror from the front, from the sides, making sure everything was in place.

I closed the box. Now Marianne needed my attention. A new life awaited her. There was just a little way to go. It wasn't far off.

2

The doctor didn't know why it had gone wrong. It was only after the intervention that he could even begin to analyse it and approach any kind of certainty. It happened in a second, triggered by a word without meaning or coherence, a word spoken by Marianne as she was about to put down a card – things took a turn. Something died in her eyes. We couldn't get it back. An abyss opened up before me.

It was almost night by the time I left her side. Another nurse took my place by the bed so I could go to the toilet. The usual deceptive calm had descended over the corridor. The day had gone to sleep, and the night, with its own antics, hadn't set in yet.

I pushed open the door and stepped into the quiet darkness. I was alone. Barely anyone came in here for the toilet. We'd got used to holding it in. This room was for other things.

Without turning on the light, I went to the window and opened it wide. I closed my eyes, propped my arms on the windowsill and let the cool air caress my face. I stayed like that for a few breaths.

I'd kept some images in my head for moments like these.

Bibi giving me a small radio for my birthday. She'd rescued it from a dustbin and repaired it herself. Wilm and I stealing jam from the neighbours' cellar after our parents had locked us out of the flat for the night. Sarah placing her coat around my shoulders. Her scent, enveloping me. Knowing it will be fine. Everything will be fine.

There was a chair in Marianne's room, as in every room. I sat there after the intervention. My focus was on her and her alone. I'd been released from my other duties. My duty was to be there, to keep my eyes on her at all times. I don't know why it felt like a punishment.

Again and again, her body showed fleeting signs of vitality. It groaned, sweated and twitched. These were common after-effects. If I'd been less experienced, they would have given me hope. At least they kept me occupied. In between, Marianne lay there, neither awake nor asleep, her eyes looking nowhere. Sitting with her during these phases was the hardest thing I had to do.

At the end of the usual shift, someone brought me apples, a few slices of bread, and coffee. And then it was night. Apart from a trip to the toilet, I didn't leave the room.

Marianne was valuable. I realized this not just because she got all my time. I saw it in the care with which the doctor took her by the hand and talked to her. And finally I saw it in his despair. He barely let it show. He cleared his dry throat. 'It's unfortunate,' he said. 'This shouldn't happen.' Then, 'There are always setbacks. We mustn't delude ourselves. Things get better and, from time to time, much, much worse.' That's what was driving him on: the setbacks will pay off in the end, they're just the price of progress. He could hold on to that. And it was supposed to drive me on too. But when I repeated the words, alone in the room with Marianne, saying them quietly to myself, they led me straight back to the abyss. I fell silent.

He didn't yell. He didn't throw things around like other doctors did when their anger escalated to the point where a brief eruption of violence was their only release. The doctor followed the dictate of silence as diligently as we did. But I saw it in his folded arms. I saw it in the way he was always nodding. Nodding as he shone the light in her eyes. Nodding as he spoke to her. Nodding, he said, 'I'll come back in half an hour.'

Like me, he stayed in the hospital that night. He closed his office door and asked not to be disturbed unless it concerned the condition of his most valuable patient. Maybe he had the same talent for sleeping as some of the older nurses, who held on to the banister, closed their eyes and dozed a little. Maybe he phoned Ellerbach, tried to prepare him for the sight of his daughter.

Her father. He hadn't waited for her. Although he'd promised to. I could testify to that. His hand on his daughter's cheek as he said goodbye: 'When you wake up, I'll be there.'

There was a chair by Marianne's bed. We waited for her father or mother or one of her brothers to come

and ask me to stand up so they could sit by her in place
of me.

We waited.

Shortly before she was brought into theatre, I'd said to her,
'Marianne, once you get through this intervention, we'll
finish our game.' It was important to keep something for
afterwards. I did this with all of them.

During the intervention, we played a different game. An
easy one that wouldn't exceed her abilities and cause her
to panic. The first game her brother had taught her, the
brother who burned holes in his suits and dropped glasses
and who remained as absent as the rest of his family. All
they did was send flowers. Flowers and cards wishing her
a speedy recovery, gradually filling the room.

Every morning, I took over from the night nurses and
spent my entire shift in Marianne's room. Most of the time
we were alone. The doctor came in briefly in the mornings,
at midday and in the afternoons. He examined Marianne.
He gave me some words of encouragement. Then he left
again, closing the door behind him.

I was glad when I had a task to perform. I was grateful
when I needed another nurse and she stayed in the room
a little longer than necessary. The hours when Marianne's
body demanded nothing, neither food nor care, were a
real test.

I read to her from books she'd brought in her suitcase.
A ghost story and a book about hawks. I could picture it:
Marianne enjoying the shiver down her spine. Marianne,
fascinated by birds of prey, holding out for hours to catch

a glimpse of one hunting. That Marianne had nothing to do with the woman lying there in the bed.

I found photos between the pages of her book. I held them right in front of her eyes. One showed her with her brothers when they were all still children. One showed her with another woman, their faces distorted with laughter. Her room-mate? In the silence of the room, I lost myself in speculation.

I placed everything in her hands, the card game too. I guided her fingers so she could feel the surface of her belongings. Surely her skin remembered. Skin always remembers.

At the end of each shift, I dropped in to see the doctor in his office. I gave him an account of the hours I'd spent at Marianne's bedside. I repeated what I'd said to the night nurse at the handover.

He listened to me. He took notes. But he wasn't present. 'You can go now.' That's how he said goodbye each evening, usually without looking up from his notes. Only once did he set his pen aside after I'd stood up to go.

He folded his hands. 'Are you going back to your room-mate?'

That heat under my skin again. 'My room-mate?'

'Yes. You share a room, don't you?'

I nodded. He'd never asked me about the nurses' halls.

'Tell her to keep an eye on you.' He looked back at his notes. 'That'll be all.'

I turned round and left his office. I closed the door behind me. On the steps to the changing room, I had to grab hold of the banister. My feet were almost faster than I was.

Marianne should have been his key, said one of the older nurses.

'His key to what?'

'Money. To other rich families looking to fix their problem cases. So he can continue his research and boost his reputation.'

'No,' I said. 'It's not about that.'

She nodded and put a hand on my shoulder. I hated that about the older nurses. Their experience, which they passed off as knowledge, their arrogance towards nurses like me, who still believed in something. Yes, that was me: someone who believed in something.

3

I knew she was there. She was trying to be quiet, but if one body knows another, it feels its presence even in sleep. I opened my eyes. Outside it was still dusk. The light on those June days was inexhaustible.

'Sarah.'

She looked at me. She put down whatever she'd just picked up. 'Hello,' she said quietly. 'I didn't want to disturb you. You were a long way away.'

'You mustn't let me sleep.' Anger rose within me. 'When you're here, you mustn't let me sleep.' *You mustn't let me miss all these hours with you.*

'What's wrong?'

I only felt the tears as they seeped into my pillow. I wiped them away quickly.

Sarah came and sat by me on the bed. She ignored my attempts to fend her off with my hand. After all, she knew my body as well as she knew her own, and she saw that I needed her. She buried her fingers in my hair. 'Are you going to tell me what's happened?'

I needed a moment. I pressed my face into the pillow. And then it came out. The intervention. The incoherent word. The abyss. The room I wasn't allowed to leave. The flowers. Sarah listened, nodded. There were pauses, during which I thought I'd said everything.

'You've been in that room the entire time?'

'Yes.'

'And she was well before that?'

'No, of course not...' Then came another torrent. I tried to describe Marianne's rage. The silent blast in her body. The tide flooding in as reliably as it ebbed away. I told her about the other patients, about the hope and tranquillity when they opened their eyes after the intervention.

Sarah waited until I'd got every last word out. 'Do you remember what I told you?' she asked. 'About my friend?'

'Yes.'

She nodded again. Although she was still touching me, something within her seemed to move away in that instant. I sensed a muted irritation. 'Surely you can see,' she said, pulling her hand out of my hair and rubbing her forehead, 'that what's happened to your patient isn't just unfortunate. That there's maybe a more fundamental problem here. With the type of treatment.'

There it was again. She couldn't stop herself. I closed my eyes. The anger returned, swelling inside me. 'I'm tired,' I said.

'Okay.' She shifted away from me a little but didn't stand up. I could hear her trying to find the right words. She opened her mouth several times to speak, shaking her head each time and trying again. 'I don't understand these interventions as well as you do,' she said finally, 'so I need you to tell me whether... and be honest with yourself, whether these people really are better afterwards.'

I opened my eyes again. 'Yes,' I said. Her gaze was unyielding. The lines across her forehead. Her mouth poised, ready to question me further. How quickly the tenderness could vanish from her face.

'Always?'

I sat up in bed. She wouldn't let me sleep. 'Since when has there been an *always* in our profession?'

'Can you swear that your patients lead a better life afterwards?'

'What are you asking me?'

Something inside her stiffened. Her body suddenly felt so heavy sitting there on my bed. A weight that was pushing me deeper into the mattress too. 'I can't help feeling these interventions are harmful. And I'm not the only one who thinks so. I've read that they quieten people down. Especially women. That they take something of *themselves* away from them.'

'No,' I say. 'That's not true. That might have been how it used to be, well... years ago, in psychiatric institutions. But that's got nothing to do with what we're doing now. We don't quieten anyone down. And what is that supposed to mean, anyway? Take something of *themselves* away? Where have you been reading such nonsense?'

Sarah stood up and went to the window. She supported herself with both hands on the frame, dropped her head between her arms and took a few deep breaths. Her shoulder blades, which I knew so well, were now protruding sharply from her back. 'At least I don't believe everything someone tells me just because they're higher up than me.'

My anger towards her intensified. Anger because she refused to see what we were achieving in this hospital. Anger because of the many times I'd tried to bring it up with her and she'd brushed me off. 'You're right. You don't understand our intervention. How could you, anyway? It's impossible to talk to you about it. Do you have any idea how these people were beforehand? They were... in institutions. In prisons. They'd got themselves into hopeless situations, like the women on your ward. They were addicts, like your friend. We could have helped her too.'

She struck the window frame with her hand. She struck it hard. I fell silent. 'Help?' She turned towards me. Her jaw was trembling. 'It was their help that killed her!'

I put my feet on the cold floor. Was she about to throw a shoe? Or even give me a slap? But instead she turned back to face the window. She was withdrawing from me. That's what she did best.

'Haven't you noticed?' I said. 'All you see is her. I tell you about my work, about my patient, and you see her. You couldn't care less about the good that comes out of medicine. All you see is her.'

'And all you see is some sort of... hope.' Her voice became calm again. My hope, the hope she recognized in me, seemed to pacify her. She put her hand on the windowpane. 'You can't see the part we play in all of this. As if what we share with one another, we two, you and I... had nothing to do with it.'

'But it doesn't. It's your pain that makes you think that.' It had infected everything. It was in her eyes, in her words, in this room. An intense weariness came over me. 'It's not my pain.'

'Of course it is.' She tapped her fingertips on the windowpane. 'It belongs to all of us.'

Get up. Get up and go. Only come back when she's ready to talk about something else. There was no other way to cope. I stepped into my slippers.

'So they can cure psychological disorders now.' She nodded. 'I understand that. So it's only logical that one day they'll do that with me as well.'

'Sarah, please.' A cold weariness seized me by the throat. I needed fresh air.

'Wouldn't they say that about us two? That it's a psychological disorder?'

'They're not saying anything at all about us.' I saw the doctor before me. His folded hands. His question about my room-mate. The heat under my skin. He didn't know anything about us.

'Does he serve you coffee in his office?' She looked at me. 'Does he tell you you're something special, your doctor? You'd like to be, wouldn't you? Something special?' She shook her head. 'But you're no different from us. Do you know that? You're playing his game. But they're his rules.' She turned to me and put her hand on her chest. 'You're just like me.' I thought she was going to cry. 'Think about it. Strike out your hope, then see what you've got left.'

Get up and go. I had to leave, otherwise there'd be no end to this. I stood up and was about to head for the door, but Sarah was quicker. She bolted towards me and grabbed my arm. My skin cried out. It remembered the silent assent between our bodies. It didn't want to go.

'My friend may have been an addict, but that's the only difference between her and us. The only one.'

I stood firm against her gaze. 'You can keep your pain,' I said. 'I don't want it.'

'You can be so stupid, Meret.'

I wrenched my arm free from her grip. 'I have to go,' I said. I didn't say: *I know I can be stupid. So stupid, I'd give myself a good beating if I could.*

'Be my guest. Don't let me stop you.' She stepped to the side to let me by. All the tension seemed to fall from her as I passed. Her body softened. It softened like a body after a fight, giving in to its exhaustion. And I went, even though I wanted to stay there and take her in my arms. I went, even though my skin was still crying out, crying out as I closed the door, crying out as I went down the stairs and stepped outside.

4

'Hello?' I said into the receiver. There was a crackle at the other end of the line. 'Hello?' I said again, louder this time.

'It's me,' came through the crackling. 'Bibi.' No one else announced themselves like this on the phone. She did this with everyone she called. How often we'd tried to drum it out of her, rattling off phrases like 'This is Bibiana', or even 'Bibiana here'. 'Can't you at least say: *Bibi here?*' No chance.

I clutched the receiver.

'Meret, did you get my last postcard?'

'From America?'

'Yes, pretty cool, wasn't it?'

'And are you in America?'

'Are you crazy? How on earth am I supposed to get there? I'd have to book a seat on the deck. And on the plane...'

And on the plane you'd have a panic attack. I always forgot that. In my head, Bibi was indestructible, not someone with a fear of flying. Not someone whose stomach could be turned upside down by lurching waves.

'How are you?' Bibi asked.

'Okay.'

'I'd be able to tell all the way from America that you're not okay.'

'Nonsense.'

'Well, if you say so.'

'I'd rather hear how *you* are.'

'Really well, actually. I'm opening a café. With some friends.'

'Friends?'

She groaned. There was another brief crackle on the line.

'Bibi!' I shouted down the phone. I was afraid the call would be cut off. But she didn't seem to hear me.

'It's… a dump. Or rather, it *was* a dump. We've done the basics. We've even got an alcohol licence. But we don't have a beer tap yet. Or a water supply.'

'Where do you live?'

'What do you mean, where do I live? On the streets, of course. What a stupid question.'

'I'm serious.'

'I live in a house, like most people. What's up with you?'

'I haven't heard your voice for months. I was beginning to think I'd never hear from you again.'

Not a word at the other end of the line. 'I know,' she said finally, her tone subdued. 'Sorry about that.'

Whenever she went silent on us, I imagined she was ashamed. She was ashamed, and that's why she never called. I pictured her holding the receiver in her hand but not being able to bring herself to dial one of our numbers. Because she didn't know where to start. Where to start to make things good between us.

'Do you need money?'

'I'm earning money.'

'How?'

She snorted. Now I fell silent. In truth, I knew it wasn't shame that stopped her calling.

'Tell me about your café.'

'It's in a corner building. It used to be a… well, it looks like it used to sell sanitaryware, because when we saw the shop for the first time, there were five toilet bowls and two bathtubs lying there – just imagine! And the dust, layers of dust, I'm not kidding you, and rubble and… you don't always know what kind of stories these places have, do you? Don't you get a shiver down your spine when you think of all the stuff that went on in that hospital?'

'Yes, of course… Well, go on.' *Stay on the line. If you don't want to talk, just breathe. Just breathe into the receiver.* I swallowed my silent plea.

'Tomorrow we're going to start building the counter. I designed it.'

'That's great, Bibi. I'm sure it'll be the best counter in town.' *I know what a good eye you have. How precise you are. I'm your sister. I know you.*

'I have to go now.'

'No, don't go yet.'

'I'll call you again soon. But you have to promise you'll tell me then how you really are.'

'But the phone's in the corridor.'

She burst out laughing. 'So what? And you're a human being, or isn't anyone in the building supposed to know that? Where do *you* live, anyway?'

139

'Bibi.'

'Yes?'

'I miss you.'

'I'll give you a number. Next time I call. I'll give you a number you can reach me on.'

'That'd be—'

'But you mustn't give it to anyone else. Not like last time. You have to swear to keep it to yourself.'

'I swear.'

Was she clutching the receiver, like me? Or was my voice worth less because I wasn't going anywhere, because my number always stayed the same?

'Take care.'

'You too.'

I stayed there, the phone beeping in my ear. It took a while for me to hang up. I studied my hands. I didn't know what they were for.

I'd waited twelve days, but Marianne's eyes were still empty. She'd been transferred the previous day.

I was given only a few minutes to say goodbye to her. I packed her case and handed it to the two carers who'd come to pick her up.

After that, I made up the bed for the next patient. I scrubbed the floor. I took the flowers and shared them out between the rooms that didn't have any. There wasn't any rush, the older nurses said. But still I finished within the time frame dictated by my inner clock. It was still working.

Our room was empty too. Sarah had written me a note to say she was going to be visiting her mother more frequently and didn't know when we'd see each other next. That was the only thing she left for me. No books, no freshly picked flowers, no mess. Over the last few days I hadn't even found any of her hair.

I opened my eyes in the mornings and for less than a second she was still with me. I breathed her scent and felt her warmth still flooding the room. Then came the certainty: she hated me. When she'd said, 'You can be so stupid,' all the warmth had drained from her eyes.

The certainty sank like a stone. I stood up and went to the toilet, I relieved myself, I washed my face, I drank my coffee, I ate my porridge, I got on my bike, I set off, I was on autopilot, my body acted, I didn't have to think.

5

Not long after they'd transferred Marianne, I saw the
Ellerbachs on the front page of a newspaper one of the
older nurses was reading at the breakfast table. I asked
her to save the article for me.

Two new patients had arrived. Two more interventions
had been performed, without any complications. I kept
thinking about Marianne. The doctor said they'd chosen a
lovely place for her, and I believed him. I believed this care
home had the best beds and the best pillows, the promise
of time, more time than had been granted to other desperate souls. But I could see it all in my head: the suitcase,
the cards, the chair for visitors. All of it left untouched.
These images ambushed me whenever I started to feel sure
of myself again.

The doctor and I talked a lot. He'd call me into his
office, where we'd go over Marianne's intervention. He
didn't do this for his own benefit. It was important to him
that I regain my confidence in the procedure.

On one of these occasions, the doctor asked me about
Bibi.

'Do you know where your sister is right now?'

Something inside me contracted. The few words Bibi and I had exchanged on the phone, the postcard that had arrived for me a few days later with the telephone number on it: this information was intended only for me – that was part of the deal. So I said, 'I haven't heard from her in a long time.'

'And now you're worried something might have happened to her.' He said it with such conviction, it made me laugh. He gave me a look of irritation.

'Forgive me,' I stammered, 'it's just…' It's just that everyone, including me, had always thought the worst would happen to Bibi. Life would eventually punish Bibi, because how could it go any other way? What else was such behaviour asking for?

Happiness, something said in my head, and I couldn't help laughing again, because it was absurd, even more absurd than the doctor, who was assuming the worst. I could hear Bibi's voice, her happy voice, telling me about the café she was opening with her friends. I could feel the receiver in my hand, how I'd clutched it as if my life depended on it.

'What if it isn't true?' I asked the doctor.

'If what isn't true?'

'That we're punished for certain things.'

'What makes you think that?'

'My sister, she…' No, I thought. Bibi doesn't belong here. There was a place inside me for her alone. Why had I let the doctor in too? In my mind, I erased my sister from this conversation. I erased her from all conversations in this office in which I'd ever mentioned her. 'Let's not talk about this any more.'

'Do you think Bibiana needs to be punished?' The ground seemed to shift momentarily when he said her name. He'd memorized it when I first mentioned her, and hadn't forgotten.

'Of course not. You misunderstand me.'

The doctor leaned back in his chair. 'I don't believe in punishment,' he said, and I envied him. Of course he didn't believe in punishment. He had his certainties. He held on to them, and when they shattered, he formed new ones. 'But some things attract punishment, let's not delude ourselves. People are punished for their appearance, their illnesses – it has nothing to do with guilt. You and I, we have a part to play in protecting people from punishment.' He cleared his throat. 'That's a big statement to make, I know. But there are so many arguments for the intervention, and I see this as one of them.'

'To protect people from punishment?'

'What do you think will happen if things go back to the way they were? Even if it's only a fraction as bad. That's all it takes for people to start saying *Let this lot live, let that lot die*. You and I know full well this could happen at any time. Things are... fragile. That's what I have learned in my life.'

I said nothing. I nodded, letting the conversation taper off. He was tired. He kept glancing at the telephone. An important call awaited him. Probably his youngest daughter, who still loved him unconditionally. It wasn't like the other times when he kept talking, clinging to his words because they gave him purpose.

'It's good that you have doubts.'

'Doubts?'

'And ask questions. That's why I chose you. It takes a certain perspective, I think, a sense of what it means to carry something inside you that doesn't belong there.' He wiped his brow. 'My youngest is about to call. You can go now. Let's continue this conversation another time.'

That evening, I sat in our room on my bed and read the newspaper article. It was about the Ellerbachs opening a new factory. The eldest son was going to run it. There was a photo of him on his own, a proud man. And next to it a photo of the family – the one I'd seen in the paper several times before.

Marianne was missing. She was no longer there, standing beside her brother, where she should have been. I scrutinized the photo. I scoured the background for incongruities. I ran my fingernail along the brother's shoulder, which should have been pressed against Marianne's. Where were the traces of her having been cut out of the photo?

It was a near-perfect absence. The only thing missing was a tiny piece of the window that had been blocked by her head. 'Ha!' I exclaimed when I discovered it. A hot flood of satisfaction surged through me. And then I scrunched up the article. I sank my teeth into the paper.

6

I waited for her. It was my day off, and I lay in bed and waited for her. My heart beat faster whenever footsteps approached the door, even though I would have recognized her steps if I'd heard them among all the others going up and down these corridors.

I was waiting in vain. She must have known I was there. She was avoiding me.

It was like in the beginning: I clung to the things she'd left behind. I ran my hand over her blanket. I opened the wardrobe door and looked at her clothes. I opened her books at the dog-eared pages and read what she'd last read.

I also did things I wouldn't have dared do in those first few weeks. I climbed into her bed and covered myself with her blanket. I closed my eyes and imagined her placing her hand on my cheek, stroking my neck with her fingers and kissing me. I still felt her touch everywhere. She left me with the sensation of being nothing more than a body, a body that wanted to grasp and feel.

I pulled her clothes out of the wardrobe and buried my nose in them. I smelled her sweat. I couldn't get enough of it.

I wanted her to come back. I wanted her mess back. I'd have given anything for that.

I wanted to set her straight. The intervention had nothing to do with what had happened to Sarah's friend. Her story had made her half-blind. Surely she could see this.

But I also remembered the time before her. The reliable passing of weeks and months. My strength. The person I was before Sarah came into this room. Before she churned up my life.

I'd rather she stayed away, I thought. Her smell needs to leave this room. She needs to go, and take her emotional turmoil with her.

I had my work. I had the days, in their familiar form. I'd visit my family soon. I'd be a daughter there, a sister – I was good at that, after all. I had the suitcases. The blue box. The concertina. The flip book. Bibi's book. The cards. I just had to endure the stabs of pain. And when nothing else worked, then count. Count through the pain, the doubts, the confusion, until it passed. It always passed.

7

The phone rang in the early hours of the morning. A voice at the end of the line asked if I could come. A nurse on my ward had gone down with flu.

At this time of day the building was dead. Everyone was asleep or at work. No one had made coffee or porridge. I put some granules in a cup, poured on some hot water and gulped it down, retching on the gritty solution. I stuck an apple in my mouth and cycled off.

She was a few hundred metres from the hospital. She'd stumbled. A large sack lay on the ground in front of her. 'Can I help you?' I asked, stopping beside her.

'No.' Without looking at me, she waved me away. 'I don't need any help.'

'Are you sure?'

Now the woman looked up at me. In the near darkness, it was almost impossible to read her face. Still, I recognized something familiar. I searched my memory for what it was.

'Yes.' She'd got up again. She brushed the dirt off her clothes. She wasn't a nurse.

'Where are you going at this time of day?'

She smelled. Not of neglect, not of unwashed skin. But she smelled. 'I know your voice,' she said. She picked up the sack off the ground and slung it over her shoulder. 'You were with me when they put me right, up here.' She tapped her forehead.

A passport. I remembered a passport. 'Your name's Vera.'

'Yes.' She smiled. A brief smile that won out against the dark and then vanished abruptly.

I got off my bike. A minute, I thought. The hospital can wait a minute. 'Can I accompany you some of the way?'

'That's not necessary, thank you.' She turned away from me.

'I'd like to.'

She stopped. For a second, she seemed to be wobbling. I wanted to leap towards her and help her, but something held me back. 'Okay then.' She continued, steady on her feet.

'My name's Meret. Do you remember?'

'No.'

I walked beside her.

'We read a book together,' she said. 'I remember that.' She was disappearing under the sack on her back.

'Isn't that too heavy for you?'

'No.'

She smelled of soap. Not the soap we washed with. The soap used for cleaning vomit, pus and blood.

'Do you work in the laundrette?'

'Yes.' She patted the laundry bag. 'It fell off the van. Fresh sheets. Or uniforms. Like yours.' She was walking steadily, undaunted by the weight on her shoulder.

'Do you like the work?'

'What do you mean?'

'Do you like it? At the laundrette?' The question reverberated in my head.

'I get somewhere to sleep.' She sped up, going half a pace faster than me. 'And something to eat.'

'Do you get a wage?'

'Yes, I just told you. Somewhere to sleep and something to eat.'

She'd been a criminal. That's what the doctor had told me back then. She stole and swindled and turned violent when she was caught. She couldn't stop herself. It was an inner compulsion that overpowered her. The doctor would put this compulsion to sleep. To him, no one was too poor, too needy to be treated. He set great store by this.

'Are you sure you don't need any help?' I was about to put my hand on her shoulder, but she evaded me. Her body seemed to move away from me automatically.

'Sure.' She wasn't looking at me. I thought I saw her face twitch when I made another attempt to keep up with her. 'Please,' she added.

'Okay then. I'll go to work.'

'It was nice seeing you again.'

'Yes. Take care.'

Yes, I kept hearing as I got on my bike. It followed me like an echo to the hospital, into the changing room, onto the ward.

8

The buses to the surrounding areas set off from behind the train station. I soon found the right number. I only had to look at the smartly dressed people standing on the concrete island, laden with flowers, smoking one last cigarette before departure. It was obvious where they were going.

I boarded, paid and went through to the back. I took a seat by the window, and on the empty seat next to me I placed the bouquet the tight-lipped assistant had made. *I'm not going to see my family* had been on the tip of my tongue, but he could already tell by my face.

The bus followed the railway tracks for a few miles before turning off into the suburbs. It didn't stop for anyone at first, only taking on a new passenger once we were nearing the countryside. It was an older man, holding flowers – like all of us who were heading to the care home. His eyes wandered around the bus. Hope, I thought. He was full of hope. He was probably one of those family members who put up photos and talked about the past, determined to prove that the person he was visiting had once been fit and healthy.

Most of the people I cared for shared the same conviction: *I used to be whole.* If they couldn't express this themselves, their families did it for them. The past was a condition, a place so unspoiled it would have barely withstood translation into reality. But everyone wanted it back nonetheless.

I used to have two legs. I used to have a regular heartbeat. I used to be able to see. I used to stand under the shower on my own; I'd put my head down and let the water rush over it until I'd had enough. I'd get out. I'd dry my hair. I'd gather up my clothes and put them on. I'd make myself a coffee. I'd lock the door. I'd go down the stairs. I'd step out onto the street. I'd take a bus.

It wasn't always like it is now.

That's why there had to be a way back. People who'd once been healthy – you couldn't just abandon them to hopelessness. People clung to hope.

I placed my hand on my stomach. The motion of the bus was starting to get to me. That wasn't normal. I didn't usually feel travel-sick.

Closing my eyes, I tried to resist the urge to get off the bus. In my head, I started counting.

He was different to his siblings. It wasn't his size or physique, or the way he spoke. They all spoke in the same way – it was a language they were made of, the cloth they were cut from.

'Thank you for coming.' He extended his hand towards me. 'How did you hear about it?'

There was something about his body. You couldn't tell

from the photos in the newspaper, but I saw immediately, now he was standing before me, that it was too large, too proud for him. That he didn't feel at home in his skin. That the gestures he'd learned were impeccable but they didn't belong to him.

'Hear about it?' I reached for his hand. Over his shoulder was the photo of Marianne and her old room-mate. It was framed and stood on the table by the wall. Did he think I was her?

'My family are doing their best to make my sister disappear from the face of the earth.' He stepped to the side. 'Come in, take a seat. Can I take those flowers off you? I'll put them with the others.' He gave Marianne a gentle shake on the shoulder.

'Look,' he said, 'you have a visitor.'

There was no change in her condition. Her eyes were only half-open. Her gaze travelled past me into the void. But I thought I saw a flicker of surprise in it.

'Hello.'

I considered touching her. That would show her I was really there. But my hand only made it halfway. Before I could touch Marianne, I lost my strength.

'It's nice here.'

The doctor hadn't been lying. The place was a world away from the usual hopelessness of such institutions. But it had been easier in the preceding weeks. Easier to tell myself I'd visit Marianne than to actually set foot in this building. I owed her a visit – I'd become convinced of this. *And what do I get out of it?* she asked me in her stillness.

I averted my gaze. I looked at the table with the flowers on it.

'I know it must be a shock. How long has it been since your days at boarding school? And now she's lying here like this…' He put my bouquet into one of the empty vases. 'I was shocked myself. But you get used to it.'

'This kind of thing doesn't frighten me. I'm a nurse.'

'Really?' He studied me closely. Suspicion cut in between us, but then his smile returned and it fizzled out.

'Yes.'

'How did that come about?' He was genuinely curious. He couldn't imagine why I'd take up this profession of my own free will.

'I wanted my own life. And a vocation.'

He nodded. He remembered why I was there. 'What do you know?'

'Everything there is to know. I think.' I looked at Marianne again.

'They say there's not much hope. They say she's gone. That the only thing still functioning is her body, because it's trying to stay alive. But that's not true. She knows I'm here. She also knows you're here. You can see that, can't you?'

'Yes.' Hope is dangerous. I'd seen how it could ultimately drive people to despair. But there was no alternative to it. Not on my ward. Medicine, after all, stood on the shoulders of hope. I had to keep it alive, no matter how desperate the situation.

'I'm sure the two of you will be able to go outside again soon. You did that a lot at boarding school, didn't you? You sneaked outside so you could watch people?'

'Yes.'

He was already picturing it. I didn't want to take it away from him. I didn't want to be like the doctor, whose eyes filled with pity when I came to him to ask about Vera.

We would release people into a future worth living; this, after all, was the motivation behind the intervention. Did this future include working yourself to the bone in a laundrette? I'd asked. 'We make these people fit for work again,' he'd said. 'We give them a place in society. That would never have been possible before.' He'd slid forward a little on his chair. 'Why are you asking? What else were you expecting?' He'd waited briefly for me to reply, but then decided to carry on talking. 'And what's wrong with the laundrette anyway? You know very well that there are others who can never make this leap. I don't understand you.' He'd leaned back again. Folded his arms behind his head. He'd never done this in my presence before. For a moment, he'd looked like all the other doctors. Almost as if he'd seen this ordinariness reflected in my eyes, he'd immediately unfolded his arms again. Placed them on the desk. He'd watched me waiting, waiting silently, until he'd thought of what to say to me: 'You can go now.'

Her brother stepped up to the bed again. He tucked a strand of his sister's hair behind her ear. He studied her. He probably realized that the picture in his head didn't match the reality. His mouth narrowed. 'Sometimes I get so angry when I'm here.' His hand clenched into a fist. 'I get so angry, I kick the wall. Or smash things.'

'I can understand that.'

'Really?'

*

I smashed a cup. The day before they transferred Marianne.

I'd sat with her, as I had every day before that. I'd tried to tell myself this wasn't an unusual task. We nurses sat with the dying. That's what we learned. We learned that our presence was sometimes all we could give. And how much it meant. We learned to recognize that change in the air. Sometimes we turned our backs to the dying, just for a moment, and they'd use it as their time to go.

But it was different with Marianne, naturally. Because she wasn't actually dying. She was just lying there. My presence was worthless. I might as well have been a coat hanging on the door.

It was a momentary rage. I didn't feel it coming. It broke the surface as I was standing by the table, reaching for one of Marianne's books so I could read to her. Instead, I grabbed my cup and threw it against the wall. There was a clatter.

I looked at the shards on the floor. I looked at Marianne, who'd twitched slightly but was now lying there as still as ever. I looked at the hand I'd thrown it with. I wanted to smash more cups, windowpanes, wanted to kick the bed, the door, scream at Marianne, *Why are you doing this to me?*

Astonishment displaced my rage. My hand dropped down. I was out of breath. Ashamed.

'I've brought you a book.'

I was alone with her now. Her brother had kissed her goodbye.

'Look, Marianne.' I showed her Bibi's old book. 'I know it's not something you'd normally read… but the thing is, I think this book is a bit like a door…'

I fell silent. I'd dared to think it quietly to myself. But now my cheeks were reddening at such naive nonsense.

9

When Bibi was still very small, she sleepwalked only as far as the kitchen or the toilet. As she got older, she would wander barefoot down the stairs, sometimes even outside onto the street. Where did she go? I never had the impression it was anywhere peaceful. She would feel the furniture and objects around her, constantly looking for something to hold on to.

'Come back, Bibi.'

The book was our mother's idea. I'd seen her one night on the staircase. I woke up, saw that Bibi's bed was empty, and crept out into the corridor. Through the half-open door of the flat I could make out two figures in the dark, a smaller one on the landing and a larger one a few steps above her.

My mother was reading about mountains, and a vixen who got caught in a storm in her hot-air balloon.

'Come back.'

She extended her hand towards her daughter. At first, Bibi didn't react. She was trying to open the window on the staircase, but her sleepy fingers couldn't work the handle. Our mother kept on reading. She read with her deep, warm voice, a voice you could feel in your own chest.

Her reading opened a door. Bibi slowly and tentatively turned round, wherever she was, and walked towards this door. I didn't dare breathe as I watched the two of them. Not even once Bibi had grasped our mother's hand and let her take her in her arms. Those were precious moments in her embrace. Only rarely were you allowed close enough to hear her heart beating.

'There you are now. There you are.'

People would try anything if the prospects were bad enough. They'd throw all reason and rationality to the wind. They'd believe charlatans, turn to the stars, take up prayer, and hurriedly switch gods if theirs didn't come to their aid.

Sooner or later, they'd give up. But if they were holding books in their hands, if they were telling stories they believed would bring people back to life, you just had to let them.

We were preparing a patient for the intervention. She'd come from an institution, where she'd spent the past six years of her life. She was very sick. The type of patient of whom the doctor would say, 'We can get her functioning again. We can spare her the worst.'

And it made sense. As the doctor had said, it made sense. And when we explained the intervention to them, the family saw this too.

Her parents were already old. Her sister was there as well. She was waiting in the corridor with her grown-up son.

'Fine,' said her father, once we'd discussed everything. He took the consent form, took one last look at his daughter, and signed.

The doctor and his assistants were the first to take their leave. He'd see the family again tomorrow, and then something new would begin. That's how he always concluded these meetings with families.

I asked the family if they'd like to stay a little longer. They thanked me, but declined the offer. Like almost all the family members who brought their relative to the hospital for the intervention, they wanted to leave quickly and only come back when everything was over. I accompanied them to the stairs. I shook their hands.

'Is there really nothing to worry about?' asked the sister as I was saying goodbye. She held on to my hand a little longer.

'She won't be a burden to anyone any more,' I said. This usually allayed any final doubts. I nodded at them.

The sister released her grip, but she didn't take her eyes off me.

'You shouldn't expect her to be an entirely new person. We do what we can within the bounds of possibility. That's all we can do.' I turned away.

'Come on,' said the sister's son softly, but she stayed where she was. I could still feel her gaze upon me. It held the same scepticism as Sarah's. It followed me as I walked away. It would follow me for the rest of the day, all the way to the nurses' halls, all the way into sleep. How tired it made me.

I turned round to her again. 'It won't heal her.'

The next morning, as I was about to take over from the night nurse, the doctor asked me to come straight to his office. The woman's family had provisionally withdrawn their consent for the intervention. They were asking for more information. They wanted to meet patients who had already had the intervention. My words had been a warning to them not to blindly follow their hope.

Coffee was brought in. The doctor said, 'I understand you. But I can't tolerate this kind of behaviour here. I must put a stop to it before it escalates.'

The corners of his mouth were twitching. I recalled the fear I'd once had that he might like me. My fear of his smile. But it was just the pain in the corners of his mouth. And you only saw it if you were close enough to him.

'I knew I was taking a risk.' He took a sip of coffee. He didn't usually do this. He always let his coffee go cold in my presence. 'I was aware this might happen to you.' He looked straight at me. 'You're human, after all.'

I was thirsty. I reached for my cup. It clattered on its saucer. I withdrew my hand.

'I'm going to have you transferred to another department. Maybe it was just too much here. This will give you an opportunity to sort yourself out. And after that, we'll see.'

I nodded. There was nothing else I could do. My courage was of no use to me in here.

'Other hospitals have had a lot of success,' he said, 'with disorders like yours. Inclinations no human should have… such things don't have to go untreated. I'd like to start offering that here too. Maybe it could also be a solution for you. I'd like to help you.' Then he stood up. He extended his hand towards me. 'I'll enquire as to how you are doing.'

I reached for his hand. 'Goodbye,' I said quietly.

He blinked.

10

It happened. Nurses had arguments and had to leave their ward. I'd assumed nothing like that would ever happen to me, of course. And when it did, I waited in vain for my dismay to set in.

I was transferred to the ward on the second floor. My old room-mate had done her training in internal medicine there. When she first started, she would go very pale whenever she talked about work. It was rough, she said. The older nurses ran a strict regime. They didn't think much of compassion. Not towards anyone.

It was still like that. You could see it in the way the younger nurses climbed the stairs and lined up for the handover. That was the power of the older nurses. That would be my power one day too.

I didn't mind. I was used to it. By now I could read the older nurses. I knew the signs and reacted automatically. I didn't even feel the fear I was supposed to feel. I was under observation. The doctor had said he would enquire as to how I was doing on the new ward. Yet I was wholly indifferent to this observation. 'Yes,' was all I said to the older nurses. I did what was demanded of me, without resisting or buckling under pressure.

I changed dirty sheets, I tended to wounds, I administered medication, I washed bodies, and if I was berated and barked at while I worked, I felt no shame. I simply waited until the nurses had finished their tirade. They were as bound by time as I was. It never lasted long.

Only the night shift was a challenge. The silence breathing down your neck. The weariness, usually around three o'clock, a hammering weariness driving into your eyes and legs, subsuming everything. Death, sneaking up from behind. I could barely keep it at bay.

At the end of the shift, I sat in the changing room on the bench. I thought about the young man who'd developed a severe fever. The weariness had long since evaporated. I was on an early-morning high, rejoicing that he had survived.

When I looked up, Sarah was there. Standing only a few metres away.

We stared at each other in disbelief. The night had left its traces on us: Sarah's apron was smeared with blood, her uniform edged with dark patches of sweat.

'I heard what you did.' She came over and sat down beside me. She stretched out her legs. 'With that patient who was here to be operated on.' She took out her cigarettes and lit one. 'It was stupid.'

She blew out the smoke. So she was one of those who left their cigarette butts here – the ones we complained about and cursed because they couldn't wait five more minutes to smoke outdoors. Impossible, I thought. She's impossible.

'Please don't do anything like that again.' She was careless with her cigarette. The ash was dropping on her apron. 'I can't lose anyone else.'

How much I loved her. For a moment I couldn't breathe.

11

Once every two weeks, I visited Marianne. I did my hair before each visit. I cleaned and polished my shoes. I borrowed a handbag off a nurse from a better home. She adjusted the collar on my dress. She pulled the handbag out of the crook of my arm and moved it to the right place. She spotted every detail that exposed the person standing before her. Unlike him.

He was always there. He seemed almost delighted when I came in the door. 'Hello!' he said, looking like all he wanted to do was throw open his arms and embrace me. But he'd been trained out of such habits. He put all the emotion he felt into his handshake instead.

'Hello,' I replied. We'd never introduced ourselves. It was probably too late for that now.

'Marianne,' he said, kissing his sister on the forehead. 'You have a visitor.' He let me have his chair. He stayed standing, but seemed to crumple as all the joy drained out of him.

A strange change had begun. Marianne was starting to look as if she was made of stone. Her eyelashes, her nails, her mouth, her skin – her body seemed entirely untouched by time in this bed. He, on the other hand, was starting to disappear. He'd become thinner, his face narrower, his voice quieter. The presence he'd been given, a presence to fill any room, had shrunk to the point where it no longer exceeded himself. The only thing that roused him was the joy he felt when I came. And when he talked about Marianne's progress, which no one but he could see.

'How is your work going?' he asked.

'Very well, thank you.' I didn't say: *There's been an incident. There's been a derailment on my part. And since then, I've been doubting who or what I am.*

'I play cards with her,' he said. He pointed to the pile of cards by the photographs. He told me this every time. He said he followed her blinking, or the tip of her index finger. That she'd already won a game this way. And then he forgot, and told me again.

'Has she had any visitors since I saw her last?' I asked.

'You know what they're like.' He frowned briefly. The furrows in his brow seemed to be saying: *No, you don't know what they're like. You don't know anything about us, you're not one of us.* Then they vanished again. 'Father has expanded the foundation. Now he even pays for scholarships for working-class children. Have you read about it?'

I shook my head.

'He would roll up his sleeves and single-handedly drag anyone out of the dirt. Apart from us, of course. After all, we're his own. He'd have to take a good look at himself in the mirror. And grapple with what he sees there.' He cleared his throat. 'But what am I saying? You're here. You've come all this way. The day you left, Marianne was distraught. Of all the places you could have gone to when you left school, you chose the middle of nowhere.' He sounded reproachful. 'Did you get married there?'

'No.' Her old room-mate had moved in with her sister. A tooth as a farewell gift, and Marianne never heard from her again.

I was grateful. I was grateful that here, I could step into her shoes. That I could be her for a few hours. That here, I wasn't worthless. I could be useful if I wasn't me.

Her brother accepted my *no*. 'There's a doctor here,' he said, 'who's trying a new treatment. He's cautiously optimistic.'

'What kind of treatment?'

'A high-dosage drug. High enough to' – his hand made a fist and thumped his chest – 'restart someone's heart.'

'Who is this doctor?'

He went over to the table. He poured two glasses of water but only brought his own back. 'My father asked me the same question.' His water went down the wrong way, and he coughed. 'He phones here, did I tell you that? He asks me to hold the receiver to her ear so he can talk to her. He tells her about his day.' He wiped his mouth with the back of his hand, then screwed up his face as if there was a bad smell in the room. 'I'm the spitting image of him. More than my brothers and sister. The nose, the eyes, the mouth, the ears… everything. I even sound like him on the phone.'

'I wouldn't get the two of you confused.'

'You definitely would.' He smiled, and he became a different man. 'But thank you for saying so.'

His smile was infectious. It was all over this room. I looked at Marianne, convinced it would infect her too.

'Tell me what you know about this treatment.' I wanted a taste of this hope he was still harbouring. I knew I shouldn't. Not me. I knew better. But I still wanted it.

12

She opened the door as I was getting changed. 'Sorry,' she said, closing the door in front of her a little.

'Come in.' *You've seen me before, haven't you?* I added in my head.

'How was your night?' She slipped into the room behind me.

'Long.'

'Mine too.'

We saw each other more often now I had night shifts on the new ward. We said goodbye to each other in the usual way: 'See you Saturday.' 'See you Monday.' 'See you next week.' The familiar untidiness was returning, and in the corner stood our plant, showing off its luminous green, unperturbed by anything that had happened in this room.

'Have you eaten yet?'

'No.'

'Shall we go down and see what there is?'

I nodded. We'd only recently started doing that together again. 'Sure.'

Glancing over my shoulder, I saw she was still wearing her coat. She was waiting until I was done and had moved away from the wardrobe so we wouldn't get too close to one another. Since we'd gone back to living in the room together, we'd avoided closeness, any physical contact.

'Meret,' she said softly.

My heart leaped. She'd said my name, breaching the invisible boundary between us.

'I'm all done.' I sat on the bed and undid my ponytail. My scalp hurt. I massaged it with my fingertips.

'You are being careful, aren't you? About what you say to people?'

'Of course I am.' I didn't say: *Actually, I couldn't care less what happens at work any more.* I'd said this to her once before, and it had enraged her. Through clenched teeth, she'd forbidden me to repeat it.

'What's on your mind?' She pressed her palms together.

I looked over at her. At first, we'd also avoided any eye contact. I'd reacquainted myself with every corner, every spider in this room so I didn't have to look at her.

'An encounter.' Now she was looking at me too. My body stiffened.

'What kind of encounter?'

The image of the young woman was before me again. The laundry bag, the sparseness of her words. It wouldn't go away. 'She was a patient of mine.'

'Did she have an intervention?'

I nodded.

'And she survived it?'

I nodded again, this time more energetically. 'Everything went fine. We discharged her three days later. Then...' My chest was burning. 'Then, her new life began.'

'What do you mean by that?'

'Now she works in the laundrette. I met her when she was bringing laundry to the hospital.'

'Right.' Sarah rubbed her palms together. 'And how was she?'

'She was…' I shook my head. I saw Vera's clothes before me, folded and stowed under her blanket in hospital. Her small, light suitcase. Her face twitching while we were talking, as if she was suddenly afraid of me.

'Do you remember her name?'

'Vera.'

'Vera.' Sarah folded her hands together again. She's enclosing this name in her hands, I thought. Now it can't escape again. A childish defiance rose within me.

'I worked with time,' I said, 'as the older nurses taught me. But I don't understand… They said I just needed to carry out my duties, every day, and eventually I wouldn't see the individual faces. I'd see the bigger picture. Time would be on my side.'

Sarah was silent. She stood up.

'Isn't that how it's supposed to be?' I asked, my voice brittle with defiance.

'No.' She shook her head. 'No, it isn't supposed to be like that at all. I… I'll never forget my patients' faces. What makes you think time is on our side?'

Something tightened in my throat at her tone. Everything in this room was fragile. Every word, every movement. If I pushed too hard it would be over. I said nothing.

She put her shoes in the wardrobe. It still didn't bother her that everyone else took off their shoes at the entrance.

171

Sarah walked around the halls in her shoes, tramped up the stairs in her shoes, thundered down the corridor in her shoes, no matter what the other nurses said.

Sarah took off her coat. She still wasn't wearing a scarf, hat or gloves, though the weather had turned cold.

'Do you still hear from him?' She pulled off her stockings and threw them into the wardrobe.

'He sends his regards, once in a while.'

'Regards.' She took a few steps. 'Regards,' she repeated quietly, stroking her lips with her fingers.

'Do you miss it?'

'Yes,' I admitted.

'Your conversations?'

'I miss sitting in his office and knowing that… things are possible.'

She stood still. 'I can understand that.'

'Really?'

'Do you think I'm not capable of vanity?' She shook her head. 'You should know me by now.'

Yes, I knew her. I knew her body so well. Every day, I missed touching her.

'Come on,' she said. 'Let's go and get something to eat.' I stood up. I followed her out of the room, along the corridor, watching her hands. The hands that had enclosed Vera's name.

13

He phoned me on a Sunday morning to tell me Marianne was dying. 'She should have been better by now,' he said. I could hear the anger in his voice.

Over the past few weeks, they'd been giving her the experimental medicine. The drug was in use in other clinical areas. In an extremely high dosage, it was expected to gradually wake her up. But instead of waking her, her body, which had remained functional, was now gradually giving up.

'Please come,' he said. And immediately retracted it. Now, with death so close at hand, I no longer had any business there. The family would slip back into their roles; they would be mother, father and brothers again, ready for a proper farewell, proper mourning. *Family only* was the rule on these occasions. Only the people she belonged to. 'So it's all been a waste of time.' He gulped. 'Thank you,' he said quietly. 'Thank you. You were there. Thank you.'

After he'd hung up, I went into our room. I sat on my bed and looked out of the window. I couldn't look at Sarah's bed.

On my final visit, I'd told him who I really was. He'd nodded. 'Yes, I'd already guessed.' And for him, that was that. In her room, this secret had no power at all. I realized he welcomed any visitor who came through the door. Anyone who would shorten his solitude with her by a few minutes.

Days or weeks. That was all Marianne had left. And when it was over, her hair would keep growing for a while. Of its own accord.

I readied myself for the news. I believed it would bring me a sense of relief.

Briefly, I'd been able to share her brother's hope: Marianne opening her eyes, and everything being exactly as it was before the intervention. Except her rage wouldn't wake with her. Her rage would simply stay asleep.

I quickly relinquished this image. All I could picture was visiting Marianne, Marianne in this persistent state, forever. I had no idea how she was. Maybe she wasn't so bad. What did I know? After all, wasn't it me feeling the warm weight of her life and wanting to be released from it?

Five days later, he called again. I rushed to the phone, still in my nightdress. This time there was no anger in his voice. He was flustered. He didn't sound like there'd been a death.

'My sister would like to see you,' he said.

14

There was still something untouched about her, a quality that had only set in since her body had found its new state. But there was also unease. Maybe it scared her to know that this body didn't need any input from her to keep going. That it was built to function and wouldn't let her go if it was capable of this.

'Hello,' I said.

'You took your time.' Her voice wasn't her own again yet. Her words sounded stilted, as if she was speaking an unfamiliar language. She put her hand to her larynx. The vibrations in there must have felt strange.

I stayed standing by the table.

She pointed to the chair beside her bed. 'Sit down.' Then she hesitated. 'Please,' she added, unsure whether in here she should be asking me to do things, rather than ordering me around.

Up close to her again, I saw the cracks in her skin. Fine lines branching across her cheeks.

'My brother told me you were here.' She pointed to the table by the window, where the flowers stood. 'Apart from you two, only plant life comes to visit.'

'Do you remember?'

'Remember what? You, here?' *What we did to you*, I wanted to say. Instead, I nodded.

'Maybe.' Her fingers felt for her larynx again, resting there as she carried on speaking. 'Sometimes images come into my head. Like in a dream you remember at some point during the day. A very long, very tedious dream.'

I looked over at the cards on her bedside table. 'Your brother played cards with you here. He told me about your games. Do you remember?'

'He played cards with *me*?' She snorted. 'With himself more like – what an idiot.' She grabbed the cards and dropped them on the floor beside me. 'He left me on my own. For years. He pretended it was a law of nature. He was a brother and I was a sister, and these were... two different worlds.'

She was breathing quickly. It took almost all her strength to talk. I wanted to calm her down. Place my hand on hers. I wanted to tell her about Wilm. That my brother had gone, too, off into a different world. I said nothing.

'It's still there,' she said after a while, her right hand clutching the sheet. 'It's still in me.'

'What is?'

Only now did I notice the photo frame. It was standing on the bedside table. Her and her family. The glass was shattered.

'Your rage?'

'They said I was lucky. That people don't usually come back from that kind of thing. That it probably won't last long. They said that too. But they have a lot to say. They know everything. Apparently.'

'If I can do anything…'

She shook her head. She didn't want to know about my guilt. 'I hoped it would go away. That I'd wake up and… I wouldn't feel the rage any more.' She looked at me. 'The doctor was here.'

'Here?'

'He sat there, where you're sitting. He said if things improve… if things stay the same… with me… we can try it again.'

'No,' I stammered. My voice could barely manage that one word. 'No,' I said again. My neck went cold. I tried to imagine the doctor here at her bedside. His words, which always made sense, which were his greatest skill, greater than anything his hands could accomplish.

'Fine by me.' She nodded. 'I don't want to go through it again either.'

My eyes filled with tears. I wanted to open her hand and place myself in the hollow of her palm. I wanted to cry for her.

'Get me out of here.' There was something about her that wouldn't let you turn away. Not when you were sitting so close. 'Take me somewhere. I don't care where.' She pulled back the blanket from her hip. There were marks on her thighs from all that time spent lying down. 'As long as it's away from these rooms, where I'm… sick… and damaged.' She let go of the sheet.

I was trapped by her gaze. 'I can't,' I said, forced to look her straight in the eye.

15

She was sleeping. I wanted to go over and wake her, but I just stood by the table. I leaned on it and watched her.

I'd got up that morning before she was back. I'd gone to the toilet, had breakfast. A night shift lay ahead of me, so I had the day to myself. I'd run some errands. I'd sat outside a café. I was the only one out there in the cold eating a slice of cake.

'Sarah?'

She didn't react. A few months before, I would have woken her by kissing her eyelids. I remembered exactly how her skin felt on my lips.

'I want to ask you something.'

She nodded drowsily.

'Shall we take Marianne away?' I moved over to the bed and propped my arms on her mattress. 'We'll make a plan, and then we'll go.'

She stared at me. For a moment, she didn't seem to know whether she was dreaming or not.

'Let's go, Sarah.'

She shook her head, confused. I took a deep breath so I could say everything in one go before she had the strength to answer back.

'We'll drive away from here, and we'll never come back. All we need is a car. You can drive, can't you? And a place to go. And a plan, of course. We'll need a plan.'

Now she was wide awake. She grabbed my hands. 'Are you mad? What are you talking about? We can't do that.'

'Why not? Because we have duties?' Agitation in my body. Excitement running through me, all the way to my fingertips. 'Because it's wrong? Because we'd be punished?'

'Because it's...' Her voice died away. She gripped my hands with force, in a way she hadn't touched me for months. 'Because it's...' She shook her head again and fell silent.

Without her, without her I could live in peace.

'Are you serious?'

I nodded. She pressed my hands to her mouth. I thought she was going to kiss them. But then she rested her head in my palms.

16

It was almost dark when we set off. We passed through the suburbs in silence. Sarah didn't trust a single green light. 'See if anything's coming,' she instructed me at every junction. Otherwise she said nothing. She navigated us through the increasingly rural roads. She'd memorized the map. She said that when it came to finding the way, she trusted no one but herself.

We were early. We parked at a slight distance and waited. Sarah switched off the engine. She opened the glove compartment, took out her cigarettes and stuck one in her mouth.

'Can I have one too?'

'No.' She wound down the window. She pulled a packet of mints out of her pocket and handed them to me. 'Here. If you want to get addicted, try those.'

We sat like that for a while. Sarah smoked a second cigarette, then a third. By the time the fourth was in her mouth, the desire had passed. She threw it out of the window.

She'd bought the car three days before. We'd pooled all our savings. It had already done a lot of miles with its previous owners, too many in my opinion. But Sarah was sure it would get us to our destination. She said she knew a thing or two about tin cans. She could always tell if they would let her down.

'Do you think she'll come?' It was already twenty minutes after the agreed time. I realized I was hoping. For a few seconds, I'd hoped we could drive home again and slip back into our old lives.

'Let's see.' Sarah leaned back. She seemed very calm, but her heart was racing. I saw it thumping in her chest.

She'd kissed me. After she'd bought the car, she'd come into our room, taken my face between her hands and kissed me. 'We're really doing it.' She'd pulled me onto her bed. She'd rested her forehead on mine. 'We're really doing it.' Then every movement had seemed automatic. Her neck. Her armpits. Her stomach. Her legs. The warmth between her thighs. Her eyes on me. Her gasping. The sounds the pillow could barely stifle. Her exhausted body, which almost dissolved in its embrace with mine.

I didn't want to go back.

She took one hand off the steering wheel and tousled my hair. 'It'll be fine.'

As long as we're together, I added silently. I took a few deep breaths, closed my eyes, sucked in the cool air. Our car smelled of leather and smoke. Our car, I thought, and my fingertips tingled with warmth.

'They're coming.' Sarah let go of my hair and turned on the ignition. Through the window I saw two figures approaching the car. Marianne's brother was pushing her in a wheelchair. Her legs weren't strong enough yet. It had only been a few weeks, not enough time to build up her muscles. Months lay ahead of her, ahead of us, before she'd be able to walk that far.

'Good evening,' said her brother, shaking Sarah's hand. His formality was almost comic. Marianne gave us a nod, a thin smile playing on her lips.

Her brother helped her onto the back seat. He embraced her. After shutting the door, he put his hand up to the window. She pressed against it from the other side. Then he knocked on the bonnet. 'Take care,' Marianne said softly. Her lips tightened.

In the rear-view mirror, I saw him crumple. Not like others, who fell to their knees, threw themselves on the ground and sobbed. He was an Ellerbach, after all; his composure was greater than he was.

We drove almost all the way back. The closer we got to town, the more I sensed the growing unease within me. Sarah had insisted this was the best route. No unnecessary detours that would add hours to the journey. I put my hands on my knees. I tried to imagine Sarah's heart. Its beat.

'We can turn around any time,' I said to Marianne when we got to the station and took the road heading out of town again.

'I know.'

She'd told her brother he owed her. For all the years he'd left her on her own. She would forgive him. If he let her go.

'I know.'

Marianne soon fell asleep, so Sarah and I were alone as the lights petered out around us. 'Would you like me to talk to you to keep you awake?' I asked Sarah.

'Every now and then, I'd like you to say: *keep going.*'

'Keep going?'

'Yes. That's enough.'

'I can do that.'

'Good.'

We only stopped once. Sarah made the most of the few minutes I took to relieve myself by the roadside. In the brightly lit car I saw her prop her elbows on the steering wheel, fold her hands, then close her eyes. She mouthed her prayer soundlessly.

We woke Marianne. She opened her eyes and looked at us with a calmness I hadn't seen before.

'Are you okay?' I asked. I put my palm on her forehead. 'Do you know where we are?'

'Yes. And yes. Can I go back to sleep now?'

She let us undo her belt, place her feet on the back seat and put a cushion under her head. She briefly squeezed my hand as I covered her up again.

We passed a few villages, and then there was nothing else. The headlights were all we had to show us the way. I slowly relaxed. There was the steady motion of the car, the unevenness of the road, us.

'Keep going.'

We hadn't been able to take everything. We'd argued over the plant. I said we should leave it for the next occupants, to help them make their room a home. Sarah was of a different opinion. She even threatened not to drive if the plant stayed in the nurses' hall.

'Keep going.'

I looked at the fogged-up windows and drew patterns in the condensation with my finger. I waited for the rain.

Sooner or later it would come, raindrops covering the car, propelled into rivulets by the speed.

'Wait here.'

I must have fallen asleep. I woke when the car stopped. It was still dark outside. Everything was unfamiliar.

Sarah got out. She went over to a brightly lit window, bent down, picked up some gravel and threw it at the pane. A cry of protest came from inside, and the window was flung open.

'What's going on here?' roared the woman, looking out at her daughter. 'What are you doing here in the middle of the night? I thought you were coming tomorrow!' She disappeared from the window, and we could hear her grumbling as she came down the hallway. 'Have you brought a whole caravan with you? Didn't you say... How many people did you say were coming? What do you think I am? A hotel?'

The door opened. The hall light illuminated the two of them as they embraced. I saw how tightly they held each other. How her mother placed her hand on Sarah's head, almost lifting her off the ground.

'What are you doing to your old mum?' she scolded. 'Are you trying to kill me?'

'Wake up,' I said. 'We're here.'

17

I'd imagined it would be a museum of past lives. A house full of things left behind.

I stopped in the hallway on my way back from the bathroom. I could hear Sarah's mother in the kitchen through the open door. 'I don't usually smoke,' she said, followed by the sound of a match being struck.

Above a little telephone table hung the photos Sarah had told me about. I tried to make out the faces in the dim light. Everything here was precious. Everything here was connected with her.

I could hear her rinsing our plates. I could hear the clattering. She was taking her time. I pictured the movement of her hands. Only Marianne had managed to eat more than a slice of bread since our arrival. She'd been almost talkative.

It was too dark to properly make out the photos. I turned away, running my fingers over the telephone. Sarah's voice must have come out of it so often. She always called her mother in the afternoon, said hello and waited while her mother got a glass of water, or sometimes waited longer, not knowing whether she was looking for something or sitting there in silence, staring out of the window at some detail that had caught her eye in the vast landscape.

I took a few steps and peered through the half-open doors. Barely anything anywhere, only contours. Beds, tables, lamps. I hadn't reckoned on such emptiness.

'I'm off to bed,' Sarah's mother said. 'My daughter can show you where everything is. The folding bed is in the laundry room – can you put it up in your room, Sarah?'

Marianne cleared her throat. 'Are we all sleeping in the same room?'

I couldn't help smiling. I leaned against one of the door frames and stared into the emptiness within, wishing I could sink into it.

'Yes, of course.' The sound of another match. 'Do I look like I have enough wood to keep the whole house warm?'

I couldn't yet feel the solid ground under my feet. If I closed my eyes, everything sped past me again.

The voices fell quiet, then I heard Sarah's mother again: 'You can sleep in my room with me, if you prefer?'

'Yes,' replied Marianne quickly. 'Yes, please.'

Sarah's mother hadn't expected that. She stayed silent.

Sarah burst out laughing. She choked on her laughter, coughed, struggled for air. Someone thumped her hard on the back.

Quietly, I laughed with her.

I remember our first morning together in this house.

It was still dark. She was lying with her back to me, but I could tell she was awake. She was breathing quickly. She'd realized the consequences of what we'd done.

I remember her turning over and looking at me without saying anything.

'Yes?' I extended my hand towards hers. Our old life, the one we knew our way around, the one we knew how to lead, was still very close. Our room in the nurses' hall was waiting for us. The rotas. The things we'd had no more room for.

She hesitated.

I remembered the blackness outside the window. The silence. Even the house respected it.

I didn't know how things worked here. I didn't know anything about this new life.

'Yes.' She reached for my hand. Whispering, so as not to disturb the silence, she repeated the word that would get us through the years, up to this point here and now: 'Yes.'

THE AUTHOR WOULD LIKE TO THANK:

Kaśka Bryla, Melanie Waelde and Dorothee Elmiger for reading and rereading this text, offering feedback and coming up with all kinds of suggestions. Laura Dshamilja Weber and Lina Muzur for editing this text with such dedication, intelligent questioning and patient commentary. Felicitas Hoppe for a stimulating correspondence. Julia Novacek and Hannah Martin for the many conversations about art and life, and Hannah for also coming up with the title. Julia Eichhorn and Zoë Martin for inspiration, coffee and sorting out contracts and everything else. The Strodehne crew for the unforgettable summer weeks that gave rise to my favourite passages. Carolin Krahl, Olivia Golde, Eva Schörkhuber, Jiaspa Fenzl and once again Kaśka Bryla from the *Politisch Schreiben* editorial team for all our work together, and for being there. Stella Sabin at Peirene Press and Marielle Sutherland for their meticulous work on the English translation. Anna Hetzer for accompanying me in my work and my life – I never want to do without again.

THE PEIRENE SUBSCRIPTION

Since 2011, Peirene Press has run a subscription service which has brought a world of translated literature to thousands of readers. We seek out great stories and original writing from across the globe, and work with the best translators to bring these books into English – before sending each one to our subscribers, six to eight weeks ahead of publication. All of our novellas are beautifully designed collectible paperback editions, printed in the UK using sustainable materials.

Join our reading community today and subscribe to receive three translated novellas a year, as well as invitations to events and launch parties and discounts on all our titles. We also offer a gift subscription, so you can share your literary discoveries with friends and family.

A one-year subscription costs £38, including UK shipping. International postage costs apply.

www.peirenepress.com/subscribe

'The foreign literature specialist'

The Sunday Times

'A class act'

The Guardian

PEIRENE | STEVNS
TRANSLATION PRIZE

The Peirene Stevns Translation Prize was launched in 2018 to support up-and-coming translators.

Open to all translators without a published novel, this prize looks to reward great translation and to offer new ways of entry into the world of professional translation.

The winner receives a commission to translate a text selected by Peirene Press, the opportunity to spend two months at a retreat in the Pyrenees and a dedicated one-on-one mentorship throughout the translation process.

The Peirene Stevns Prize focuses on a different language each year and opens to submissions from October to January.

With thanks to Martha Stevns, without whom this prize would not be possible.